The HOUSE of Three SISTERS

VIRGINIA NIELSEN

SCHOLASTIC BOOK SERVICES
New York Toronto London Auckland Sydney Tokyo

Cover Photo by Owen Brown

ISBN 0-590-32416-0

12 11 10 9 8 7 6 5 4 3 2   2 3 4 5 6 7/8

Printed in the U. S. A.   06

The HOUSE of Three SISTERS

A Windswept Book

WINDSWEPT TITLES
FROM SCHOLASTIC

Don't Walk Alone by Mary Bringle
Someone is Out There by Carole Standish
Girl in the Shadows by Miriam Lynch
The House of Three Sisters by Virginia Nielsen

CHAPTER

1

IT was lonely that night after my mother left on her honeymoon with Kelly Porter. It was strange, too, sleeping in my mother's bed instead of making up the sofa bed in the living room. Sometime in the night I awakened from the old nightmare about my father.

Tiger thumped his tail twice as I got out of bed but did not stir from his rug, which I had moved to the bedroom so he could be near me. Barefoot, I crossed the carpeted floor to open the drapes at the window of the motel apartment where my mother and I had lived since my father's death. I stood there in my pajamas in the dark, looking out over the valley, while my heart slowed to a normal beat.

"You should be helping me pack for *my* honeymoon," I'd told my mother that afternoon.

"Oh, Janice!" For a moment she looked startled. Then she laughed. "Your day will come."

"I thought you would never forget Daddy. I thought that was why you didn't want to go back to our house in Champaign. Or did you decide to stay in California because you had met Kelly?"

"Honey! You know we couldn't throw Professor Albertson out before his lease was up."

I said stubbornly, "It was only for the summer quarter. And that was last summer."

It was not that I didn't like Kelly Porter; I did. But it was not yet a year since that terrible day when a swimmer came running into the coffee shop, dripping water all over the carpet, where my mother and I were having breakfast.

"Do you think I've forgotten, Janice?" my mother asked, sharply. She straightened up from the suitcase lying open on the bed and laced her fingers together the way she does. My mother has beautiful hands. "You don't stop loving someone when he dies." She paused, then smiled at me. "Not even if you fall in love again."

Don't you? *I* haven't gone looking for another father. Somehow I'd managed to keep the cruel words back. In spite of her irritation with me she had looked so happy, like she was singing inside.

And now she and Kelly were together.

I stared out of the window in the dark predawn. The motel sat on a little elevation above the road to Mt. Eustis County Park. It was somewhat isolated, but within driving distance of her job and my school in the valley, and it was so much cooler up here that my mother had been happy to find a one-bedroom apartment available next to the manager's apartment. Below the road, the pines and oaks were masked in shadow. Over them, a thin slice of the valley, misty pale, reminded me of the distant sea in my nightmare.

I was back at Morro Bay in just such a motel room as this, looking out at the black silhouette of "The Rock," fifty acres of it, marking the boundary between bay and ocean. Between that dark rock and the pale sand below my window, the water of the bay was a glittering black.

The bay. Deep and mysterious. I had seen it in every mood last summer, under every kind of sky. There are fish in its green depths. Sometimes there are whole schools of fish. The cold current flowing south along the coast is diverted by The Rock into the bay. Like leaves before an autumn wind, the schools of tiny fish are swept into its pocket.

Often in my dreams I saw them, silvery flashes moving in precise patterns below the surface. After them came the big fish, dark shapes turning and rolling in the inky green depths . . . sharks, following the current south, discovering in a frenzy of gluttony the schools of fish caught in the pocket of the bay.

I shivered.

Last year a migrating gray whale had followed a school of sardines into the bay and was trapped. I often dreamed about him, swimming around and around, forsaken by his companions, unable to find his way out. Eventually, he had washed up on the beach below our window . . . to die.

Tonight I had dreamed I was the whale. I wondered if there would ever be a time when I would sleep peacefully again, without nightmares.

"I will never forget your father, Janice," my mother had said, folding her plaid dinner skirt. "If I had had another child, do you think I would have stopped loving you?"

"That's different." My voice had unexpectedly thickened.

She had smiled, shaking her head, a quirky sort of pitying smile that always infuriated me because it was meant to remind me that I was too young to understand. "No, it isn't all that different, dear. But it's cold sleeping with a memory."

I guess I can understand that. What I didn't understand, then, was why she was so worried about leaving me alone here on the Mt. Eustis road. Could she have guessed how lonely I would be, even while I was glad to be on my own?

I stayed at the window until the sky lightened and the valley became squares of cultivated land surrounding the cluster of miniature buildings that was the town of Santa Teresa. Then I crawled back in bed and slept until Tiger nosed me awake, asking to go out.

The Mt. Eustis Lodge sits on its small bluff with a balcony connecting the units and a wooden stair running from the adjoining coffee shop down to the road and parking lot below. In back of the units, there is a higher-level service road and more parking spaces for the permanent residents. That's where my mother's car was parked. My car, for six whole weeks.

While I slept the sun rose, bringing wisps of fog rising from the floor of the valley to obscure its grid of roads and canals. Tiger lunged past me as I opened the door. Mrs. Crowder stood in her open door just on the other side of the wall that separated our units. She was wearing a watermelon pink robe. My mother can wear watermelon pink but it was absolutely mad with Mrs. Crowder's brassy hair. Tiger planted his forefeet on the deck and barked at her.

"Keep that damn dog quiet, Janice," she hissed. "People sleep late on Sunday, you know."

"Quiet, Tiger!" I ordered. "I'm sorry, Mrs. Crowder."

"You going out?"

"Tiger needs his exercise."

"Well, don't go far."

So it was going to be like that for six weeks. With exaggerated patience, I said, "I've been taking Tiger for a walk every morning since we came here, Mrs. Crowder."

"Yeah. Well, just be careful, honey. You can't tell who might be wandering around in them trees. We had a degenerate once, an escapee from the crazies' hospital down the state. You never know."

Ugh. Was she going to be popping out of her door every time I opened mine? I remembered my manners and said nothing more, but I was furious. I had Tiger's leash snapped on now and we edged past her and started down the steps.

I had stubbornly insisted that I could stay alone while my mother and Kelly were combining his business trip with a honeymoon.

"A baby-sitter!" I screamed when my mother wanted to get someone to stay with me. "What would Greg think?"

Greg Baxter is a year older than I am; he is going to USC next year, but I have another year at Santa Teresa High. Greg lives in Santa Teresa, but in the summer he is a park aide in Mt. Eustis County Park. It's ironic that my summer intern job is in Santa Teresa. And naturally, being a park aide, he works most weekends!

"I'm going to be seventeen," I told my mother. "I have my driver's license and a job. And I have Tiger to protect me. What more do you want?"

What she wanted was Mrs. Crowder, not only willing but able to pop out of her door every time I opened mine.

I crossed the road and walked through the trees until I found the hiking trail that wound up the mountain. There I let Tiger go, following him at an easy pace. Invisible birds shrilled warnings of our coming. Bright blue butterflies fluttered in the dappled sun along the path.

Tiger was already out of sight. The air was both mild and tangy with the scent of pine and the dry crushed needles under my feet. Behind me the trees had swallowed the bluff and everything on it except the red glow of Mr. Crowder's neon sign which read BAR AND EATS.

In summer the valley is like an oven and when the warm air meets the air from the ocean over the coast range, it lays down a heavenly cool mist in the mountain valleys in the early morning. I could see it through the trees below the trail, settling like fog in the hollows.

I don't much like Mrs. Crowder. "There'll be a few ground rules, honey, and I want that understood," she said as soon as my mother and Kelly drove off in Kelly's old Thunderbird. "There'll be no parties, no drugs and all that jazz. That good-looking boyfriend of yours kisses you good night *outside* of your door, period. Got that?"

"We're not making out, Mrs. Crowder," I said, with dignity. Sometimes Mrs. Crowder is gross, absolutely gross.

"She's pure brass, just like her hair," I'd told my mother. We both know she tints it.

"She is a good-hearted woman, and she has been especially nice to us," my mother reminded me. "I expect you to be nice to her."

Well, it was better than having her living with me. Just barely.

I slowed and whistled for Tiger. I couldn't see him but far ahead of me he began barking furiously. I took a deep breath and started running again.

Around a bend in the trail I saw them, a man and a woman — and my dog circling them purposefully. "Stay, Tiger!" I shouted. We were usually alone on the hiking trail mornings like this, and Tiger thought we owned it.

He stopped barking when he heard my voice, but he sat on his haunches, alert and poi ed, facing the couple. They stood still, laughing good-naturedly as I ran up, breathless, with my headband slipping and my hair sliding about my face. "Heel, Tiger!" I ordered, grasping his collar.

"Why, it's Janice Litton!"

I looked up at Marita Folsom. With her was Tony Kapel, one of the partners in the engineering firm in Santa Teresa where my mother works. Marita is her supervisor. It had been Marita who arranged my summer intern job in the typists' pool there.

"It is Janice, isn't it?" Marita's warm, laughing voice brushed formality aside. "Is your dog really a tiger, Janice?"

"Sort of," I admitted, and an odd flicker tightened her smile. Another person afraid of big dogs? "I'm sorry," I apologized. "I usually have him on a leash when there are people around."

"Sometimes a dog has to run, eh, Tiger?" In his windbreaker, his shoulders hunched, and his cheeks reddened with exercise, Tony Kapel looked younger than he did behind his imposing desk. "German shepherd?"

"About three-quarters."

Tony grinned. He is very attractive for an older man, with a profile strong enough not to be overpowered by a generous head of curly hair.

Marita? It's hard to describe her, especially the way I saw her then. So much has happened since that Sunday afternoon. Thin as a model, wiry and dark, quick-moving. I guessed she was about eight years younger than my mother, which would make her a dozen years older than me. Not as pretty as my mother, until Marita flashes that high-voltage smile and then — well, I had seen it happen at the office, in the room where our typewriters chattered. She would come in like a breeze of sun-warmed air, her dark head thrown back, her smile wide and wonderful, and you could feel the response flowing toward her from each desk.

Charisma? She had *something*. I wished I had it.

She had charmed Tony Kapel, the only unmarried partner in the firm. And now she was turning that voltage on me. I wondered why, but I was pleased. Already I felt less alone.

"Give Tony the leash," Marita said, linking her arm through mine in a companionable way, "and come walk with us. Isn't this a wild coincidence, our meeting this way?"

"Not particularly wild," I told her, "since I walk Tiger twice a day."

"Do you, really?" she marveled. And then she protested, laughing, "Such energy! You make me feel so old, Janice!"

"Do you live near here?" Tony asked me.

"At the Mt. Eustis Lodge."

"The motel?" Tony's voice held thoughtful surprise. I guess he thought it must be rather expensive on a permanent basis for one of his secretaries, but my mother has a small income from the house back in Illinois, which we rented when my father came to give a summer series of lectures at the Polytechnic College in San Luis Obispo. "A paying vacation," he had chortled when he took the motel-apartment for us twelve miles away on the beach at Morro Bay.

I didn't want to talk about that so I said nothing. Tony was handling Tiger as if he were used to dogs, but from time to time Tiger growled uneasily. He must have known Marita didn't like him.

"There's a restaurant and bar, isn't there, Janice?" Marita asked. "With a fireplace, maybe? I'd love to relax with my hands around a hot cup of tea."

"As a matter of fact, there is — fireplace and all." It didn't occur to me then to wonder if she were describing something she had already seen.

I walked back with them the way I had come, wondering what Greg would think if he saw us on his way to the park headquarters. As we climbed the steps to the restaurant Marita asked me, "Did your mother get off all right?"

"They left about eleven yesterday."

"Then you're all alone."

"Alone?" Tony Kapel said, lifting his eyebrows.

"I'm right next to the owner's apartment," I said, pointing out our door, and added, making

10

a face, "You wouldn't believe how well I'm going to be chaperoned."

They laughed, Marita turning to face me and pushing the lounge door in with her back. Tony reached over her tousled head to hold it for us. I thought, what an attractive couple they are.

"Is Tiger allowed inside?"

"In here, but not in the coffee shop."

The lounge was deserted. A driftwood fire burned in the corner fireplace above a raised hearth. Marita walked over to it, holding out her hands. "A pot of tea?" she suggested, answering Tony's lifted eyebrow.

"What would you like, Janice?" he asked me.

"A cup of coffee would be fine." Through the entry to the coffee shop I could see Mrs. Crowder sitting at the counter with a cup in front of her. She turned to see who had come in and her sleepy-lidded eyes widened in suspicion as she saw me with two strangers. Perhaps it was enjoying Mrs. Crowder's surprise that made me lose my self-consciousness with my two bosses. Or was it all Marita's charm?

"Come warm your hands, Janice," she urged me. I slipped Tiger's leash over the back of a chair and moved up beside her. "What a great spot! How did you happen to find it?"

"It was my father who found it. One weekend when we were exploring —" To my horror, my voice trembled. I was remembering my father saying, "We may never get back to California. Let's see everything we can while we're here." How I missed him!

11

Marita's eyes softened in immediate understanding. "How do you feel about Kelly?" she asked me.

"He's okay."

"Do you mind being alone while your mother's away?"

"It's okay," I said again. "I've got Tiger." I saw that odd flicker in her eyes again.

Tony was back, carrying three mugs in his large hands. We each took one. Marita and I sat on the raised hearth, cupping our hands around our hot drinks. Tony pulled over a chair that was too small for him and straddled it negligently. They were both so beautifully sure of themselves.

I looked out the window toward the valley, lying bleached under the morning sun, and wondered if Greg had driven by while I was on the hiking trail. I thought idly about climbing the road to the park this afternoon, on the chance that I would see him. He would probably be on the truck that drove around picking up and emptying trash cans. Maybe he would call me and stop by after work.

And what would we do if he did, when I couldn't invite him in? Darn Mrs. Crowder, anyway!

When Tony (I could not help thinking of him as Mr. Kapel, as I did at the office) and Marita decided to have brunch in the BAR AND EATS and invited me to join them, I accepted.

"I'm glad we came out here today," Marita exclaimed, happily, smiling at me. "I usually go home for the weekend."

"Home?" I repeated. "Don't you live in Santa Teresa?"

"Only during the week. My home is near San Juan Bautista."

"Your obsession, you mean," Tony teased her, and Marita laughed. "It's a Spanish monstrosity," Tony told me. "It must take all of Marita's salary just to pay the taxes."

Marita laughed again, not contradicting him. "You must come home with me some weekend, Janice, and decide for yourself if it's worth it. How about next Friday? My niece will be home from college. She's about your age."

If her niece was in college she was not "about my age," but I was flattered.

"How about it?" she repeated. "Tony is driving me over and there's room for you. Isn't there, Tony?"

"Just about," he said, smiling at me. "We're leaving after work. You could bring your overnight case with you in the morning and leave your car in the employees' parking lot."

I sipped my coffee and asked, "What about Tiger?"

"Bring him," Tony said promptly.

After the smallest interval Marita said, "Yes, of course. Bring him."

Faintly, through the hum of conversation from

the coffee shop, I heard Mrs. Crowder's deep, coarse laugh. For some reason it made me feel lonely and unloved. Why not? I thought. Greg would be working.

"Yes, I'd love to," I said.

CHAPTER

2

I stared at the telephone for a long time that afternoon, willing Greg Baxter to call, but he didn't. Before dark I took Tiger out again. Most of the Sunday visitors to the county park had gone back down the mountain, and a stillness had fallen over the deserted trail. The birds were quiet. The sun slanted through the trees, its rays filled with dust motes stirred up by the weekend hikers.

Back in the apartment I watched television for a while, laid out a blouse and skirt to wear to work, and then went to bed. My mother's perfume still lingered in the bedroom and I thought for a long time about the changes her marriage to Kelly would make in our lives. We would probably be moving down to a real house in Santa Teresa. Would Kelly find a place where I could have Tiger? He'd better! My father had given me Tiger when he was a tiny, wriggling puppy.

Before dropping off to sleep, I spent some unhappy minutes wondering if my mother would sell the house in Illinois with all its memories of our years there with my father. When Tiger wakened me, barking furiously, I thought for a few seconds that I was in my bedroom with the eyelet curtains and the shelf of dolls above my bed. Gradually the motel-tan drapes came between me and my dream.

Tiger had hurled himself through the living room to the front door and was making enough racket to waken the dead.

"Tiger, for heaven's sake!" I groaned. Rolling out of bed, I slipped on my robe and padded barefoot across the carpeted living room to let him out.

Just before I opened the door I snapped awake and really looked at my dog. He was sniffing at the crack below the door and barking in the sharp way he did when someone knocked. Through his noisy alarms, I heard the sharp calls of disturbed birds in the trees below the road. My heart froze as I wondered if there was someone out there on the balcony. What time was it, anyway?

I switched on a light and looked at my watch. Two o'clock!

"Who's there?" I called, and Tiger stopped barking to listen with me. A dead silence followed. Then Tiger growled. The skin on my arms prickled. I felt a presence. There was a body on the other side of the door. Someone was standing there, someone who was listening and saying nothing.

"Who is it?" Tiger heard the break of panic

in my voice. He sprang at the door with a heavy thud and an eruption of savage barking.

I heard sounds from the Crowders' unit and knew Tiger had wakened them. "Mr. Crowder!" I yelled. "Mr. Crowder!" But Tiger was making so much noise I was not sure he could hear me.

They could hear Tiger, all right. There was a sharp rapping on the other side of my living room wall. I suspected that was Mrs. Crowder. During all the commotion, I thought I heard light footsteps on the deck running around the coffee shop to the rear, but I was in such a panic by then I could not be sure I was not imagining it. I did not dare open my door, and I was so mortified that Tiger had wakened Mrs. Crowder that I hesitated to disturb her further.

Tiger stayed at the door for a few minutes longer, growling deep in his throat, then turned and trotted back to his rug, curled up on it and settled down to sleep. A moment later my telephone rang.

When I reluctantly lifted the receiver, Mrs. Crowder's voice, thick with sleep, said, "Janice, are you entertaining someone in your room?"

I gasped, and said furiously, "I am not!"

"Well, keep that damned dog quiet!"

I slammed down the phone. I had not realized until then just how much Mrs. Crowder disliked Tiger.

For a few moments I wondered if it had been foolhardy to insist that I would be perfectly safe alone in the apartment. But I was behind locked doors, unharmed. And hadn't Tiger frightened the intruder away? Reassured, I went back to sleep.

Greg called me the next day at work. My supervisor told me about the call with disapproval written all over her face.

"Hey," he said.

The little glow I felt at hearing his voice was dampened by knowing that Ms. Evans was still at my shoulder. "Greg," I said, as softly as I could, "you shouldn't call me here. Why didn't you call yesterday?"

"I was out of town. I went to a swimming meet."

I felt jolted. All day Sunday I had been picturing him slaving up at the park. I muttered, "How nice for you!"

He ignored my sour tone. "I'm trying out for the swimming team next fall. What time do you get off?"

"About five."

"I can get away from here at four. Can you meet me at the hamburger stand? I'll buy."

"Okay, but I can't stay long. I want to get up the mountain before dark."

"Yeah, you'd better. See you."

When I hung up, Ms. Evans said, "We have a strict rule about personal calls here, Janice."

"Yes, ma'am, I'm sorry."

"You'd better tell your friend."

"It won't happen again," I assured her, flushing with embarrassment.

I did not see either Marita Folsom or Tony Kapel that day, except at a distance. The Nash,

Simmons & Kapel Construction Company is the biggest firm in Santa Teresa, really big for a small valley town miles from San Francisco and even farther from Los Angeles. But it contracts for construction jobs all over the state — even out of the state — and its location makes sense because it keeps costs down. Besides, land and space rental is much cheaper here than in either of the large cities.

After work I drove to the hamburger stand. Some kids I knew at school were there, sitting around the picnic-style tables under the extended roof; not many of them had been lucky enough to find summer jobs. Greg got up from where he was sitting with three other boys and took me to a vacant table.

The T-shirt he was wearing was thin and close-fitting and it revealed those beautiful shoulder and arm muscles his swimming has developed. Greg has a great body. He was wearing his jogging shorts and below them his legs were straight and firm. We had met jogging. That is, Greg and Bob Tyson were jogging on the riding and hiking trail to the park last fall, and I was running with Tiger. Exercising your dog is a great way to meet people in a new town.

I liked his looks the first minute I laid eyes on him, and I could tell he liked me. When school started I found him waiting for me after my first class. Before long the girls were asking me if Greg and I were going steady.

"Are we?" I asked him.

"Why not?" he said, with his warm smile. "It makes sense."

"What'll it be," he asked me now. "The works?" He was cool about it but his eyes told me he was glad to see me.

I was over my pique. Being near him made me feel like singing, but all I said was, "Hold the onion."

I was hungry and for a few minutes I devoted myself to the cheeseburger he brought back. Greg was all wound up about the swimming meet, which he said was to let students who had been accepted try out for the college team. His blue eyes blazed with excitement and he kept shifting around on his bench and bouncing up and down, shaking his sun-streaked hair back as he told me all about it, letting his cheeseburger grow cold.

"I think I have a chance at the second team," he said. "But I've got to swim at least two hours a day all summer."

"Besides your job at the park?" I exclaimed, dismayed.

"I don't get any workout driving that trash truck all day! I've got to knock another minute or two off my time."

"Well, it's been nice knowing you."

"Hey, what does that mean?"

"When will I ever see you?"

"How about next weekend? I'll be in the park all day next Saturday and Sunday. In the contact station, covering for a ranger on sick leave."

Yeah. Surrounded by girls in shorts and

camisoles asking for information. I could just see it. Greg looked great in a ranger uniform. "I was up there all this weekend," I said, pointedly. "All alone because Mom and Kelly left Saturday. And I had a prowler last night."

"Well, don't be a sorehead, I couldn't help —" His eyes widened. "A prowler?"

I told him about Tiger waking me in the night and about thinking I heard someone running down the deck and around to the rear of the building after the Crowders began pounding on their wall.

"Tiger's probably over-protective because you're alone. You could have imagined the whole thing, Janice."

"Well, I didn't!"

"Just the same," he said thoughtfully, "I don't like it," and my heart lifted at his concern. "I don't like your staying there by yourself, especially on weekends. Look, I'll come out next Saturday night and stay late." He flexed his biceps. "If the guy comes back —"

"Uh-uh. Mrs. Crowder thinks it was you."

"She *what*?"

"You should hear her, Greg. She's gross. I'm off limits until Mom and Kelly return. Besides, I'll be in San Juan Bautista next weekend. Or near there."

"What's the attraction down there?"

While I was telling him about Marita's invitation, his scowl spread all over his face. "Aren't you getting out of your league?"

I had been pleased, thinking maybe he was

jealous, but now I was annoyed. "What's that supposed to mean?"

"Aren't they a little old for you? They're your bosses, aren't they?"

"What has age got to do with anything?" I asked, hotly. "I like them!"

"Yeah. But why did they ask *you*?"

That made me so furious that I put down the rest of my cheeseburger and stalked out.

CHAPTER

3

M Y first sight of Casa de las Tres Hermanas
(Marita insisted we call it by its Spanish
name, which means The House of Three Sisters)
was through the iron bars of a locked gate at
the end of a narrow road.

It was almost dark. Tony turned the beam of
his lights through the grill of the gate and they
illumined a graveled drive, curving up through
a wild tangle of overgrown garden. At the end
of the drive I glimpsed the arches of a long
Spanish gallery, and above them, second-floor
windows barred with wrought iron. Even in the
dim light I could see that the adobe walls were
dingy and flaking, but the building looked
immense.

"Is that your house?" I said, impressed. An
irregular tile roof gave me the idea there might
be enclosed courtyards. "You must have fifty
rooms!"

Marita laughed. "Most of them are boarded
up. It's the casa of the old ranch, all that's left
of my great-great-grandfather's land grant from

the Spanish governor when California was part of Mexico."

"Wow! That old?" It was gloomy with all those overgrown shrubs crowding it, and the ghostly bare trunks of the peeling eucalyptus trees in the background. For some reason it gave me an eerie feeling.

"Not the house. The original ranch house was the foreman's in my grandfather's day." She dug in her purse for the gate key which she handed to Tony.

Startled quail flew up as our tires jolted over the graveled drive. The smoky odor of eucalyptus was strong.

"It's a jungle," Marita admitted. "We simply can't afford gardeners. Rick prefers to call it natural gardening."

Tony chuckled, "It's natural, all right."

I wondered who Rick was, but did not ask.

Tony turned off his motor and abruptly the area before the entry was flooded with bright light. As we got out of the car, the front door opened and a girl with long blonde hair ran across the tiles under the arches and threw her arms around Marita.

"Sandy," Marita said, her voice warm, and embraced her. Then, "This is Janice."

Sandy looked at me with frank appraisal. Her skin was a smooth olive color, and her eyes were remarkably like Marita's. Now that they were side by side, I could see their Spanish heritage.

"And this is Tony," Marita said, above Tiger's

frantic barking. Tony had let the dog out of the car and was holding his leash taut.

Sandy's eyes lit with approval, and for a moment I saw Tony as she must be seeing him — not as my boss with the quiet aura of strength, but as a good-looking man with rugged appeal.

"Welcome to Casa de las Tres Hermanas," Sandy told us, with a radiant smile. I was drawn to her and my spirits rose.

"Where's Rick?" Marita demanded.

"In the wine cellar. I hope you're hungry. We've got a big spaghetti casserole."

"Wonderful. Tony, I'll send Rick out to help you with the luggage. You talk to Tony, Sandy. I'll show Janice to her room. It's ready?"

"Immaculate." Sandy winked at me.

"I'll walk Tiger," Tony offered, as I hesitated.

Marita led me through one of the dark arches, across the blood-red tiles, and through a massive carved door with a wrought-iron bolt. The spacious entry was tiled, as was the enormous room I glimpsed to our left. It was a living room furnished in heavy Spanish oak. A young man was walking rapidly toward us through the inner arch that separated it from the entry.

I caught my breath. I had never seen anyone so incredibly handsome except in the movies or on television. The trouble was he knew it. He moved with the arrogant grace of a dancer — or a Spanish matador, I thought unexpectedly.

Marita put her arm around me and said, "See what I brought you, Rick?"

"Marita!" I protested.

"She can blush, too," he said, with a lift of his eyebrows at Marita, and he smiled at me.

It was a fascinating smile. His long upper lip formed a straight, narrow line, hinting at firm self-control, but below it there was a pure voluptuous curve of surprising fullness. He had a faun's eyes, too, large and liquid and faintly turned up at the outer corners.

And the way he held himself! He reminded me of an old Spanish portrait of a proud young nobleman I had seen once in a museum. I couldn't decide whether he was younger or older than Sandy. As his smile deepened at the corners, I became aware that I had looked too long. I turned away, flushed and strangely confused.

Marita was laughing at me. "We're teasing you, Janice. Come on." She led me toward a curved stairway, saying over her shoulder, "Tony's outside with our bags."

"Right, Mar," Rick said, and left us.

"Just get into something comfortable," Marita suggested, opening a door in the long upper hall for me.

"I'm comfortable in this," I said, looking doubtfully down at my sweater and slacks.

"You look divine, but haven't you got something long, like an 'evenings-at-home' thing?"

"I've got a zippered robe. It's sort of a caftan. Do you mean something like that?"

"Why not? I'm sure it's very becoming."

As a matter of fact, it was.

"We'll probably eat in the kitchen," Marita said, carelessly, as she left. "Fifteen minutes?"

I relaxed, beginning to enjoy myself.

My room, like the room I had glimpsed downstairs, was spacious and severe, furnished with a few large pieces of what looked to be very old Spanish furniture. There was a marble washbasin in an alcove and, what made me laugh, a toilet behind a curtain in a dressing room almost as large as our living room at the lodge.

After Marita left me, I opened the heavy dark-red draperies and discovered that, just as I had hoped, my windows looked down on an inner court. But it was a rather depressing sight. There was a dead fountain in the center, and the stunted citrus trees in stone jardinieres around it looked half-alive. The circle of grass seemed scanty and, in the light that streamed down from my window, quite brown. The windows of the rooms across the court were boarded up. Yet I could imagine it in its heyday with Spanish señoritas, with their fans and mantillas, and bowing cavaliers gathering around a sparkling fountain.

I had just freshened and changed when I heard the scratch of Tiger's feet on the hall floor, and a knock at my door. Tony laughed at the way Tiger put his forepaws on my shoulders and tried frantically to kiss me. "I'm next door and I'll be ready to go down in five and a half minutes."

I nodded, laughing, still trying to quiet Tiger, as Tony closed my door. I had brought along the old bath mat, worn soft by countless launderings, which was Tiger's special nest. When I had spread it beside the high bed and settled Tiger on it, I stepped to the mirror. There were some decorative old pins on a tray in front of me. On an impulse I twisted my hair and knotted it on top of my head. It made me look almost as old as Sandy, I thought.

When I left my room, Tony stepped out of a door down the hall. His eyes swept down my long caftan. "You look smashing in that, Janice."

It was all I needed to give me the confidence I lacked. "Thank you, Mr. Kapel."

"Tony. We're not at the office now." He smiled at me.

He was charming away from the office. I wondered why my mother had not fallen in love with him instead of Kelly. They were both large men. My father had been a slender, scholarly man with a gentle manner and a smile so sweet it was like a knife-thrust in my heart to remember it. Neither Tony nor Kelly was anything like him, but Tony had a smooth sophisticated courtesy that reminded me sometimes of my father.

Kelly was like an overgrown farm boy. Redheaded, freckled — there were even freckles on the backs of his big hands! He moved with a kind of awkward grace that made you afraid he was going to knock a lamp off a table or trip over a rug, although he never did. Actually, he had an ease that only looked awkward, especially since he treated my mother as if she were a delicate crystal goblet.

Was that what she loved?

"What do you hear from your mother?" Tony asked, as if he could read my thoughts.

"They were in Santa Barbara two nights ago. She's catching up on the best-sellers while Kelly calls on his customers. She . . . she sounds happy."

Our motel is right on the beach, she had written. I shrank from imagining them sharing a bed.

"Kelly's a great guy, and I hear he's a terrific salesman."

Kelly had a large sales territory for a pharmaceutical manufacturer, so he probably was good. But I didn't want to discuss him with Tony.

"Isn't this a fabulous house?" I said as we descended the stairs together.

"Yes, indeed. There are probably twenty rooms, maybe more," he told me. "They use only the front block and the kitchen wing. That's roomy enough. Rick's been holding it down alone since Marita has been working in Santa Teresa. He's probably glad to have Sandy home from school."

"Don't they have help?"

"On an occasional basis, I would think. Except for the old vaquero who used to take care of the horses. He has a cottage somewhere on the grounds."

"They have horses?"

"Not anymore. Taxes must be eating them up. But it's Marita's passion; she won't give it up."

"I can understand why."

"Can you?"

I was not sure what that or his odd slanted look meant, so I just said, "It's fascinating."

The living room was still deserted, but Tony took me through it, turning right, down a long, tiled dining gallery toward the kitchen, from which we could hear voices and laughter. I gasped with delight when we entered.

It was a Spanish kitchen, immense, lavishly tiled, with old copper pots hanging from great iron hooks in the ceiling and on the whitewashed adobe walls. The room seemed full of people lounging around the large fireplace, on the raised hearth, or in leather-seated chairs.

Sandy began introductions, and soon I was able to sort her guests into two young women who had recently opened a small gift shop of handcrafted items in San Juan Bautista — Dorothy and Katherine Croft, obviously sisters; Weldon Armer, a serious young lawyer from a law firm in Hollister that Marita had apparently once worked for; a young man she called Jerry, with a long, rather plain face and unmanageable yellow hair; and a cherubic older man who answered to the name of Paul and who twanged the guitar on his knees in a chord of greeting for me.

"Tony has been telling me about the house,"

I offered, after a small silence in which they all seemed to be looking expectantly at me.

"Did he tell you it is my obsession?" Marita mocked, and everybody laughed as at a family joke.

"But what a lovely one, Marita. Did you inherit it?"

"Yes. It is half mine."

"Rick and I inherited our mother's half," Sandy explained.

"The front half," Rick put in, and again everybody laughed. Their friends were obviously well acquainted with the house.

"Were you and Sandy's mother the 'hermanas?'" I asked Marita.

"No. It was named for my grandmother and her sisters when they were young. There were three of them, all beautiful, and they had quite tragic lives."

"It was a very large rancho at one time," Rick told me. "There were other buildings then — storehouses, a bunkhouse for the vaqueros, even a private chapel. They're all gone now except the stables, where old Carlos lives."

"It's too much house for us, of course." Marita shrugged. "If he dared sell it for taxes, the county assessor would evict us. Meantime, we keep hoping Sandy will marry a millionaire."

"How crass can you be?" Sandy muttered, wiping a strand of long hair from her eyes.

"Sandy's our group project," Paul told me. He cocked a wicked eye. "Isn't she, Jerry?"

"Me, I'm working on making a million dollars," the yellow-haired man said.

Sandy joined in the hoots of laughter, but I thought I could see a faint blush creeping up her throat. It made her seem vulnerable and I felt a kinship with her. She *was* near my age.

Paul struck a few chords on his guitar and began singing a Spanish song in a thin, reedy voice. "*Canta de las Tres Hermanas*," he interrupted himself to tell me. " 'Song of the Three Sisters.' I always sing it for new guests at the rancho."

His thin voice quavered on the high notes and broke on the low ones, but Paul sang with such obvious enjoyment that no one cared. Tony whispered to me that he was a writer of Wild West stories whose hobby was early Spanish California history, the days of the great ranchos, when the presidio at Monterey was the seat of government.

I had never been in a group like it before, amiable and relaxed, made up of friends of widely different ages. Just friends, unless Jerry and Sandy were into a romance. And, of course, Tony and Marita. But now that I had met the others I was not sure whether that was a romance or not. Marita spread her radiance equally on Weldon, the lawyer, and on Paul, whose hair was getting thin on top. The gathering seemed to me both sophisticated and mature, and I had to pinch myself to be sure I was part of it.

Paul picked up his guitar and struck up a lively Spanish rhythm which set our feet to tapping. Marita moved gracefully into the clear space before the fire, arms raised above her head, and Rick followed with a rattle of his heels on the tile. Marita had wound her long hair on top of her head and fastened it with a Spanish comb. In her long ruffled skirt and black low-necked sweater, the instant impression she gave of a Spanish dancer was striking.

The music that came from Paul's guitar was very different from the gentle folk songs Greg sometimes played for me. It was loud and passionate with an exciting Spanish flavor. While his fingers flew and his foot tapped the lively rhythm, Marita and Rick stamped their feet and rotated around each other in a traditional dance that was disturbingly intense. Their eyes never left each other, and Marita's held a glittering excitement. The way they were suddenly oblivious to everything but each other made me uncomfortable, I did not know why.

But I forgot my strange unease when Rick whirled Marita out of the circle to my side. They were laughing, breathing hard.

"You were marvelous!" I told them.

"Want a lesson?" Rick asked me, as Paul began another rhythm.

"Oh, I couldn't!"

But Rick put firm arms around me and swept me into dizzying circles in the small clearing the others left on the tiled floor. The room spun around us. I clung to Rick, feeling the strength and warmth of his body. He held me, laughing, until Sandy cried that the spaghetti was '*al dente*' and we must eat it.

"It means 'firm to the tooth,' or not over-cooked," she explained to me.

We served ourselves from the huge copper pots on the tiled stove. As I carried my plate toward a chair, Marita, walking beside me, said, "You look older with your hair done up like that, Janice. It's becoming."

Behind me Rick murmured, "Mmmm, I like older women," and then I felt his lips brush the back of my neck just below my upswept hair. I twisted away so sharply my plate tilted and Marita, laughing, saved me from dumping my spaghetti on the floor.

I sat down, ruffled and upset, both by Rick's arrogance and by Marita's laughter. For a moment I wished I were back at the park, trading wisecracks with Greg and sharing a cheeseburger with him in the lodge coffee shop when he came off duty. Then Paul struck up another tune on his guitar.

It was an evening I would remember, I thought later, as I climbed the tiled stairs after bidding Marita's friends good night. Certainly I had never experienced one quite like it before. It was apparently their passionate interest in early California history and in Marita's old casa that held the group of such different friends together. The relaxed informality appealed to me. I had learned a lot in just one evening. It would be rather fun — and flattering — to be counted one of them.

I was so bemused that I was in my pajamas before I was aware of Tiger, awake and unobtrusively wagging his tail before the door. "You want your bedtime run!" I slipped my coat over my pajamas, took his leash, and went out into the dark hall.

Fortunately, a light still showed from the living room. As I descended, I was aware of voices coming from the kitchen area. They stopped abruptly, and Marita's high heels clicked along the dining gallery. "Who's there?" she called.

"It's me, Janice. I'm taking Tiger out for a few minutes."

She stopped on the far side of the living room. Tiger started toward her and Marita shrank back. "Okay, hon. I'll lock up after you." She retreated to the kitchen and Tiger bounded back as I opened the front door. Whoever was with her said nothing — it had been a man's voice — Tony?

I stood under the arches, breathing in the fragrant night air while Tiger made a few desultory runs. The "jungle" looked even more mysterious under moonlight, but I did not feel a menace from it now. Somewhere there were orange trees blooming — or was it lemon? The mixture of their heavy perfume with the sharp tang of eucalyptus buds created a fragrance that said unmistakably, "California."

Tiger was still running about, nosing the ground. Through the other pleasant night odors I caught a whiff of the wood smell of the kitchen fireplace. Paul's music and our easy laughter seemed to linger in the air. Could it be Paul in the kitchen with Marita, talking in those low conspiratorial tones?

Why had I thought of them as conspiratorial? It could be love talk.

Or it could be Rick. They could be talking family business. There must be a great deal to look after in a place like this, and Marita was away all week. There could be many reasons why they wanted privacy.

To my right and to my left, the diminishing arches made beautiful patterns of moonlight and shadow. I breathed deeply and whistled Tiger back.

Loudly enough to be heard in the kitchen, I said, "That should do, fella. Those rabbits will be there tomorrow." I went up the stairs with firmly planted steps.

Later, after I was in bed, I heard a car start up and drive away. It had not been Tony Kapel in the kitchen with Marita then, I thought drowsily. Or Rick.

I was almost asleep when Tiger lunged at my door and began furiously barking. I started up in terror. Then, as I heard soft footsteps going down the hall, I realized someone must have walked by my door. Was it the memory of my prowler at the lodge that made me imagine whoever it was had paused and turned my doorknob?

CHAPTER

4

I was wakened by a tremendous clap of sound that brought me up from my pillow and Tiger leaping from his bed. Over his frantic yelps there was a sudden burst of sounds — shouts, doors slamming, pounding footsteps outside my door. Through it all ran a brassy clangor that, after a few blurred, panicky seconds, I was able to recognize as the pealing of a large bell, so close it was rattling my windows.

Fire?

I groped for the light beside my bed, hastily wrapped myself in my robe and fastened Tiger's leash. Holding him firmly beside me, I opened my door and stepped out into the hall. It was empty, but doors stood open along its length. There was no smoke.

Lights burned downstairs. Tiger strained against his leash, still barking. I let him drag me after him, down the stairs, through the living room and dining gallery to the brightly lit but empty kitchen. The door to the kitchen terrace stood wide open.

Where was everybody?

An outside lamp spotlighted the path to the rear of the house. The early morning was dark and chill and I pulled my robe closer around me and started down the path.

Abruptly the clamor ceased, the last bell note quivering to a long musical sigh. At the corner of the building where the light ended, I paused. I could hear voices and after a moment I saw the movement of flashlights. They seemed to be going away from me into the trees.

Tiger was still barking in that sharp rhythmic way that never seemed to tire him. One of the wavering lights turned and started toward me. The others disappeared.

"You can stop that now, Tiger," I scolded. "It's all right, it's only Rick."

He was running lightly toward me on bare feet, clad only in a pair of cotton trousers, his body gleaming dull gold as he came under the light.

"Were you frightened, Janice?" he called. "Don't chew me up, Tiger! You know me, don't you, mister?"

Tiger responded with more impassioned barking, punctuated with threatening growls, and Rick stopped, eyeing him warily.

I was embarrassed. What was the matter with Tiger? "Quiet!" I ordered. "It's all right. What was that all about?" I asked Rick.

"Old Carlos in the bell tower. Let's go inside, shall we? I'm chilled."

From a hook just inside the door Rick took a sweatshirt which he pulled over his head, muffling his voice as he explained, "The old man had a nightmare. Something about a fire. He was still half-asleep, mumbling about giving the alarm."

"Where is the bell? It sounded as if it were right outside my windows."

"The tower's over the old ballroom. I'm sorry you were awakened."

"You mean there's a bell tower on the house? And a *ballroom*?"

Rick laughed. "I forget you don't know the Casa. Come out with me tomorrow morning, and I'll show you. The bell was used to summon the vaqueros from wherever they might be working to help fight fires. There were some disastrous forest and brush fires in the early days of the rancho. California's dry summers are always a fire threat, even today."

The phone shrilled, and Rick picked it off the wall. "Hello? . . . No, no problem. Old Carlos got into the bell tower. He'd been dreaming . . . Yes, I'm going to take care of it. It won't happen again. I'm sorry, you've probably had a flood of calls . . . Yeah, must have wakened everybody in the county." He laughed, then said, "Thanks, pal," and replaced the phone.

Giving me that intriguing smile, he said, "Fire station. Can you go back to sleep now? Do you want anything?"

"Where are the others?"

"Taking Carlos to his rooms in the stables. Marita and Sandy can handle him better than I can when he gets confused like this. Tony walked with them. How about something to drink?"

I shook my head, and continued shaking it as he asked, "Cocoa? Warm milk? Coffee? Something stronger? A kiss?"

I began to laugh. "No, thanks."

The faun eyes were regarding me with steady interest. "You look so young like this, all rosy from sleep, with your hair tousled. You look . . . seventeen?"

I laughed again. "How old are you, Rick?"

"What does it matter?" he countered. He was still studying me, and my face warmed. "I like you better with your hair up," he said, suddenly, catching it in one hand and pulling it up in a swift twist so tight it hurt. "I go for sophisticated older women."

"You said that before," I retorted, annoyed. The skin of my neck tingled where his long fingers had brushed it and it made me uncomfortable, not warm and happy like when Greg touched me.

"I'll put it up again," I promised, lightly, moving away from him. "See you in the morning, Rick."

Looking over my shoulder, I surprised a curious look of satisfaction on his face. That uneasy feeling came back. What did he think he had accomplished?

After I had unleashed Tiger and put out my light, I stood at my window letting my eyes become accustomed to the darkness. In slow seconds the sky lightened to a before-dawn gray. Now I saw the dark curve of the bell tower, an elongated dome of inky black with gray showing through its arches, rising beyond the roof to the rear of the court. Last night, when I looked down into the deserted courtyard, my eye, caught by its air of abandonment, had not gone up that high.

What a unique and fascinating place this was! But eerie, too . . . I couldn't wait to tell Greg about it, I thought, sleepily . . . but I wouldn't want to live in it.

When I opened my eyes Tiger had his paws on the bed and was whining to go out. When he saw I was awake, he licked my face and gave a sharp bark.

"Ouch!" I cried, clapping a hand to my ear. "So it's late, okay, okay!"

I had left my curtains open and the morning sun poured into the room. I washed hastily, pulled jeans and sweater on, and ran downstairs to let Tiger out. Then I followed the coffee and bacon aroma to the kitchen.

Marita was at the stove, enveloped in a colorful smock. "Hi, sleepyhead!"

The door to the sunny terrace stood wide open. Rick was going through it with a tray laden with dishes, silver, and a coffee pot.

"Am I the last one up?"

"Sandy's not been heard from."

I followed him outside. Tony was standing in the sun, holding a glass of orange juice with a contemplative air. He looked very solid and muscular in a knit shirt. He smiled at me and I murmured, "Good morning."

Tiger came bounding around the house and threw himself at Tony with yelps of joy. "Down, Tiger!" I protested. "Tony, do you by any chance carry dog biscuits in your pocket?"

We breakfasted lazily. Sandy had not appeared by the time we finished and we left a place laid for her. Tony helped Marita carry things inside, while I walked around the house with Rick to see the bell tower.

We were climbing slightly. The house was apparently on several levels and even larger than it had looked last night. We passed many doors in the adobe wall, and some small heavily barred windows. Above them a balcony ran the length of the wall, with doors opening to it from the second story and, toward the rear, a stair down to the ground.

"The house servants' quarters in the old days," Rick said. We turned a corner and he pointed above us. "Up there is the ballroom. It hasn't been used in decades."

A house with its own ballroom! I marveled again. "Oh, may I see it?"

"Someday I'll show you, if you don't mind a few cobwebs."

We walked along the rear of the building and came at the next corner to an inconspicuous door. Rick opened it with a key from his pocket, revealing a steep stairway, so narrow I had to go a little ahead. Now and then he put a hand under my elbow to give me a boost on a high step.

There was a peculiar arid odor. Something with wings, moving so fast I could not see it, flashed over my head, startling me so that I gave a little scream.

"Bats," Rick said. "They won't hurt you."

We made a turn and started up the second flight. Looking up, I could see far above us the curve of a bell, dark against a patch of sky. Another bat darted over our heads, turned, and streaked back. At last we came out on a platform. The bell was still far above us, but a frayed rope hung down from it.

"How did Carlos get in here?"

"With this key," Rick said. "Marita took it from him last night, but he could have a dozen more hidden around the place." He eyed the bell speculatively. "I'm going to have to take that rope down. Or tie it up."

He jumped up on the parapet of the open arch. I leaned against the parapet and looked over it. Below us was a court I had not seen before. It, too, looked abandoned. Centered in it was an empty swimming pool lined with dusty blue and white tiles. Drifted dry leaves were piled high in the corners, and in one, half-buried, I saw the gray matted feathers of a dead sparrow.

"I'll have to get the extension ladder," Rick said. "Maybe Tony will help me before you leave." He jumped down to stand beside me.

"Look, we can see all the way to San Juan Bautista today. There's the mission."

I raised my eyes from the disquieting swimming pool to the pleasant view. The bell tower of the old mission rose above the bluish foliage marking the old mission town, and a blob of color marked the terra-cotta roof tiles showing through the trees. Toward the north and west were the blue humps of the Santa Cruz Mountains of the coast range.

That pleasant aspect was one of the memories I carried with me when, several hours later, Marita and Tony dropped me at my car in the company parking lot in Santa Teresa.

CHAPTER

5

THAT night about nine o'clock the telephone rang. I sat on my mother's bed and picked it up. My mother said, "Hello, darling."

"Where are you?" I demanded. I had been fine until I heard her voice, but now the empty rooms of the motel unit depressed me.

"We're in San Diego in a lovely hotel overlooking the bay." Her voice was gay with an underlying note of excitement that had been missing since my father's death. "I'm looking down on a whole flotilla of navy ships. The weather is perfect and we are enjoying every minute of it. Tomorrow we're going to Yuma. We'll be back here in a couple of days. Same hotel. How are things there, dear?"

"Okay." Not for a minute would I let her know it wasn't that great to be alone. A wind had risen and I could hear it in the great trees that hung over the lodge from the hillside above it. Why did wind always sound like a person who had been crying for a long time?

"I tried to call yesterday from Santa Monica."

"Marita took me home with her Friday afternoon. I just got back."

"You stayed with her in Santa Teresa? Did Mrs. Crowder feed Tiger for you?"

"Mrs. C. feed Tiger? You've got to be kidding. We took Tiger with us. We went to Marita's ranch, Casa de las Tres Hermanas. Mom, it's a fabulous place."

"Well, I'm glad Marita is being so nice to you, dear. How are you getting along with Mrs. Crowder?"

"Oh, Mom, she is just too gross."

"Please don't be so critical, Janice. She is doing us a favor. Kelly would like to say 'Hi' to you."

"Okay." I waited, the receiver suddenly tight against my ear.

"Hi, Janice." It was Kelly's baritone. "Are you behaving yourself?"

"Are you?"

He laughed.

There was a tiny silence before he said, "I try, Janice. As soon as I finish with my customer calls we're going down into Mexico. What would you like us to bring you?"

"A chocolate whip."

"A what?"

"One of those things you rotate between your hands to whip up your cup of chocolate."

"Ummm," he said, and I felt a small triumph. He didn't have the least idea what I was talking about.

Ke

do."

I had a

the slender

couldn't suppre

My mother cam

to Tiger, who barke

"It was very sweet

you," she said, finally. "I'

honey, we'll call again in a d

There were so many things

her. I went over them in my mi

my clothes for morning and brush

The bats in the tower. Marita doing

dance with Rick. The plaintive tune Pau

"Song of Three Sisters." I was humming

I got in bed.

The phone rang again. I picked it up and said, "Hello?"

There was no answer. "Hello?" I said again, more sharply. "Hello?"

Tiger sensed something in my voice and began to bark. Abruptly, the connection was broken. I could hear the pounding of my heart over the uproar Tiger was making. One of the Crowders knocked on the living room wall. Angry and a little frightened, I replaced my phone.

When it rang again, I hesitated to pick it up. But Tiger gave a sharp bark to alert me, and I had to keep him quiet.

It was Greg. "Oh, it's you."

"You were expecting a call from the White House? How was your weekend?"

mother didn't leave any special instructions with me about allowing you to go off for a weekend. Does she know about it?"

"I told her last night when she called."

"You know, Janice," Mrs. Crowder said, her tone apologetic, "I've been thinking that if you wanted to invite your boyfriend in you could bring him to our apartment for milk and cookies —"

I looked at her with contempt. She thought I had gone off somewhere with Greg! "That won't be necessary, Mrs. Crowder. If you will excuse me — I don't want to be late for work."

I was furious, but once in my car driving down the hill I began to laugh. Serves her right, I thought. The meddling old hen!

Greg was waiting for me when I came home from work. He bought me a hamburger and a milk shake in the BAR AND EATS. We sat in a booth, while Mrs. Crowder sat over her usual cold coffee at the counter near the cash register, gossiping with one of the other motel guests and letting her eyes wander over to us pretty often.

Greg was not happy about my weekend, either. "What kind of a guy is this Rick?"

"He's cute."

Greg snorted. "Who else was there?"

I told him about Paul with his guitar and his rope tricks, and the Croft sisters' birdlike cries of *"Olé!"* when Rick and Marita danced, and how we ate from plates on our laps around the kitchen hearth.

"Sounds like a bunch of aging hippies to me."

"You're jealous."

"Sure I am." He grinned at me, blue eyes crinkling and neat dimples creasing his cheeks, and my heart gave a kangaroo-size hop. "You're not going down there again, I hope?" He reached over and touched the back of my hand and warmth traveled up my arm.

"I haven't been asked," I teased. At that moment I didn't really care.

But two days later everything changed. I had taken Tiger out for his morning run, before leaving for work and, as usual, he bounded far ahead of me up the winding trail to the county park. When it was time to turn back I whistled and called in vain. The pine needles quivered in the morning sun and somewhere nearby a warbler sang a few grace notes, then was still, but I could hear no rustlings in the brush, no distant yelps.

When I was becoming frantic, conscious of the minutes ticking their way to seven-thirty when I must leave for the valley, I heard a short impatient bark that said clearly, *Look!*

I lifted my gaze and there on my right, distantly visible through a gap in the trees high on the mountain slope I glimpsed Tiger, grinning down at me. He was on the other side of the county road and far above me. Why had he left the trail? He must have scared up a grouse and gone after it.

I had no time to chase after him. Enjoy the woods while you can, I thought. When Kelly moves us in to town I'll be walking you around the block on a leash. I shouted, "Home, Tiger!" and turned back.

He showed himself once again before we reached the lodge. He was still above me, on some higher trail, and his behavior was peculiar. Again he barked to attract my attention, then seemed to make a playful bound toward me as if inviting me to join him.

"Home, Tiger!" I shouted again and turned away, still keeping him in my vision. He hesitated a moment, barked once more, then bounded out of sight. At least he was headed toward the lodge. I ran swiftly down the sloping trail, confident now that he would meet me.

When I reached the motel he was nowhere to be seen. I crossed the road, whistled for him and started up the stair to the deck. Tiger came bounding through the parking lot, his mouth wide, his tongue hanging out.

"You're a fine companion for a walk," I scolded him. "Deserting me for a grouse!"

He seemed to stumble on the step above me and then just collapsed. I bent over him. Already his eyes were glazing. I slipped my arms under his shoulders and knew immediately I could not carry him to my car, which was parked up on the service road behind the coffee shop.

Tears running down my face, I shouted, "Mr. Crowder! Mr. Crowder!"

He came out of the coffee shop door in his shirt sleeves and looked down over the rail.

"It's Tiger," I called up. "He's terribly ill, Mr. Crowder. Will you help me?"

He started down the stair toward me. There was a squeal of brakes on the road, and someone came bounding up the wooden steps. I didn't realize it was Greg until I felt his presence there beside me. He looked crisp and squeaky clean in his park aide uniform, and completely competent. He lifted Tiger in his arms. "Come on," he said. "I'll drive you to the vet."

That was Greg. He had grasped the situation instantly and knew what had to be done. The shoulder muscles he had developed in swimming bulged with the strain of Tiger's weight. He said, "Mr. Crowder, will you call the park and tell them why I'll be late to work?"

"Sure, son."

"And call the animal hospital and tell them we're coming?"

"Sure. Take it easy going down the hill."

Numbed with panic, I let Mr. Crowder put me in the car and help Greg lay Tiger on the seat with his head in my lap. Then we were flying down the winding road. I cried all the way. I guess I knew it was already too late, but not once did Greg mention it.

I supported Tiger's lolling head as Greg carried him into the veterinarian's waiting room and was immediately assailed by its antiseptic odors. My dog's eyes were open but the color seemed to be fading from them. Tears were streaming down my face but I was scarcely aware of crying, so fierce was my anxiety.

The girl behind the desk took one look at us and beckoned us in past the other waiting animals with their owners. The assistant led us to an operating room and with a wave of her hand indicated to Greg that he should put Tiger on the table, then ran for the doctor.

Dr. Orcutt had given Tiger his rabies booster shot only a few weeks ago and he had said then that my dog was in excellent health. He came in briskly, a short, chunky man with a close haircut. "What happened to Tiger?"

"I don't know, Dr. Orcutt. He was fine this

morning." I described the events of the last hour.

Dr. Orcutt was preparing a hypodermic needle as he listened. "Adrenalin," he said, when he had it ready. "I'm injecting it directly into his heart."

"Is — is it a heart attack?" A sob escaped my taut throat. *I've lost my father, God, don't take my dog, too!*

"If you will wait outside I can tell you in a few minutes." Avoiding my eyes, Dr. Orcutt nodded to Greg who took my arm.

"We're in the way here, Janice."

"Save him, Dr. Orcutt," I pleaded.

"I'll do everything I can, Janice."

Two hours later Greg let me off in front of the motel and drove on to his job. I had cried all my tears and when Mrs. Crowder walked out of the coffee shop to meet me at the top of the stair all the bitter rage I felt came to a focus on her.

"He was poisoned," I said, in an accusing voice, and stalked past her.

Her eyes registered shock and her mouth dropped open, but I did not wait to hear what she was going to say. I went through my door and slammed it in her face.

In the apartment were the mute reminders — Tiger's much-laundered rug beside the bed and, in a corner of the kitchen, his plastic dishes. I picked them up and stuffed them in the garbage sack under the sink.

As I did, it occurred to me that I didn't even know where my mother was.

At that moment the phone rang and I jumped for it. But it was Marita Folsom. "Janice, dear, are you ill?"

"No. I was going to call you, Marita. I just got back from the animal hospital."

"Is your dog ill?"

"Dead," I said, flatly. "Poisoned."

"Oh, Janice, no! How did it happen?"

"I've got an idea. Mrs. Crowder has never liked him."

She didn't respond to that. After all, I remembered, she hadn't really liked Tiger, either. "I'm afraid you'll be nervous staying out there without your dog."

"Yes. Last week there was a prowler —"

"A prowler?" Marita sounded horrified. "Janice, you can't stay there alone. You pack a few things and move in with me until your mother returns. I have an extra bedroom and I will love having you. Now don't say a word," she warned, her voice cheerfully stern, "because I won't take no for an answer."

One thing I knew. I couldn't stay here under Mrs. Crowder's supervision a day longer, with this terrible suspicion in my mind. I was sure my mother would approve of my move when I could tell her what had happened. She would call again soon and if I did not answer my phone she would call either the Crowders or Marita.

I decided it was okay to go. "Thank you," I said, gratefully.

"Take the rest of the day off. I'll put you

down for sick leave. Pack the things you'll need and meet me here after work."

I packed clothes, enough for a few weeks, in a suitcase that had been my father's. After I had carried it around to my car, I came back to the coffee shop where the Crowders were at their customary stands, he behind the cash register and she at the counter with a coffee cup before her.

"If my mother calls tell her I am staying in Santa Teresa with Mrs. Folsom until she and Kelly get back."

They must have seen me walk around the deck with my suitcase, for although they looked troubled they did not show surprise.

"Sit down, Janice." Mrs. Crowder patted the seat beside her but I remained standing. After hesitating uncertainly she said, "Your mother made me responsible for you while she is away. Don't you think we had better talk this out?"

"Mrs. Folsom is a friend of my mother's," I said, distantly, "and she is extremely responsible. I am sure my mother will approve of what I am doing when she hears what happened here."

Mrs. Crowder looked into her coffee cup.

Mr. Crowder's face reddened. "Janice, my wife has her faults," he said, bluntly. "I'll admit that and so will she. Perhaps she has not handled things to your liking. But I know my wife, Janice, and I know she is not a dog poisoner."

I stood my ground and gave it to them just as the vet had given it to me. "Tiger swallowed a chunk of raw meat into which someone had inserted poison. It went into his bloodstream and running carried it quickly to his heart. He couldn't have gone far, probably only from the back door of the coffee shop kitchen to the steps where he collapsed. Those are the facts, Mr. Crowder. The doctor did a preliminary autopsy."

"My wife is not a dog poisoner," Mr. Crowder repeated. "That, also, is a fact."

The rage simmering inside me was near to erupting in tears again. "You could be right," I said. "Tiger disliked her as much as she disliked him. I don't think he would accept food from her."

Mrs. Crowder flushed. I turned and walked out.

In the car I leaned over the steering wheel and wiped away a tear on the back of my hand. Then I started the motor and put the car in gear.

CHAPTER

6

THE impersonal look of Marita's apartment surprised me. I suppose I expected something Spanish, some reflection of the Casa, but after my first startled glance around the living room — which looked like nothing more than a slightly larger version of the kitchenette units at Mt. Eustis Lodge — I realized that for Marita the apartment was exactly what it looked like: a one-night stand. Even without all the stuff we left in our house in Champaign, my mother has made our motel unit more like a home.

But although there were few personal possessions to hint at Marita's background, there were plenty of clothes in her spare closet. "You can see I've spilled over into the extra bedroom," she apologized, as she shoved some hangers back for me. "There may be some odds and ends in the dresser, too, but you'll find an empty drawer. I'll clear it all out after we eat."

"No hurry," I said, feeling rather shy. "I didn't bring much."

"Tony's coming to take us to dinner."

"Lovely."

I had just finished hanging up a few things when he came. I left the rest folded in my suitcase and hurried out of my jeans and into a skirt. It seemed quite natural now to slip into Tony's smooth car with Marita between us on the wide front seat.

"Helluva note, Janice," he greeted me, soberly, and I knew Marita had told him about Tiger. He shook his head. "I don't understand people who hate dogs."

"Tiger liked you," I said, and was glad when he changed the subject, because I still couldn't handle sympathy.

Tony took us to a Mexican restaurant in a former residence of vaguely Spanish architecture, looking like a poor imitation of the Casa's style. It was decorated with enormous straw sombreros and wildly colored pottery, and the waitresses wore ruffled blouses and embroidered black skirts.

Over our *flautas*, delicately deep-fried with guacamole and sour cream dribbled over them, I listened to Tony argue amiably with Marita, who was complaining about her financial difficulties.

"Sell off some of those dusty antiques," he advised her. "There's enough money there to pay your taxes for years."

Marita's laugh was incredulous. "Sell the Casa's treasures? Never!"

"You're being unrealistic," Tony told her, gently. "You know you can't go on supporting that huge place. You've got far too much capital invested in it for a residence, anyway."

"Oh, don't be a damn business man, Tony! The Casa is not an investment, not to me and not to Rick or Sandy. It's our home. We are Carrascos!" she said, so passionately that Tony threw up his hands in laughing surrender.

Marita laughed at herself then, but she said, "I expect to be buried on our land, Tony."

He told me, ruefully, "She will, too. Unless they foreclose for nonpayment of taxes and evict her."

"And then they will have to drag me out by my feet," Marita declared, "while I cling to every leg of furniture I pass."

"I give up!" Tony exclaimed, laughing. "I'll never wean you. But what do we do about your leaking roof? It's obviously too much for old Carlos to repair, and just as obviously it is going to ruin your treasures."

Marita's face lit up. "What are 'we' going to do? Oh, bless you, Tony! If you will help Rick and the others next weekend, I'll order a few replacement tiles. That's all it will take, you know. Just one here and there."

"That's all," Tony groaned. "Just climbing up and traipsing over those acres of tile, replacing broken ones? What a way to spend a weekend!"

Highly amused, I hummed a few bars of Paul's "Song of Three Sisters," and they both laughed.

"You'll go down with us, won't you, Janice?"

Marita asked. "We'll all work and you and Sandy can feed us."

"I'm sorry, Marita. I'm going out with Greg Saturday night."

She held me fixed with those dark eyes, bright with warm interest. "Darling, how nice. Something special?"

I shrugged. There was nothing *special* in the summertime. "A movie, probably."

"Then why don't you bring him along? We can use another pair of hands."

Tony laughed aloud. "You see, Janice? She's incorrigible."

"I'm not sure I can bring Greg. He works most weekends." That was not all I was not sure of. Greg might not want to go. But I thought how great it would be to show him the Casa. "I'll ask him."

A curious thing happened when Tony dropped us off at the apartment. I went into my bedroom, where my suitcase lay open on a luggage rack, to finish unpacking. I walked over to the dresser and opened the top drawer. It was empty except for a newspaper clipping which had been caught in the crack where the back of the drawer met the bottom.

There was something familiar about it. I dug it out and stared in surprise at my mother. She was looking up at the sheriff, whose back was to the camera. SWIMMER DISAPPEARS; SHARKS IN AREA, said the black headline above her face. The whole horror of that day was in her expression, and the nightmarish memory of it swept over me, so strong I felt dizzy.

The Coast Guard put a boat out, ma'am, and they saw the sharks. Three big ones. The one they shot was as long as the boat, a twenty-foot lifeboat. They're doing an autopsy —

I must have made some sound for Marita appeared in the doorway. "Where did you get this?" I was fighting nausea, and my voice was uneven.

Something I had surprised in Marita's eyes slid so swiftly away that I could not be sure what I had seen. What took its place was a look of deep regret. "I'm sorry, Janice. I wouldn't have had this happen for the world. But you must know that the story of your father's death was carried by the news services and published all over the country."

"You clipped it. Why?"

She hesitated. "The incident held a special interest for me. Someday I'll tell you why."

I was no longer seeing my mother's face, smudged with the print showing through from the back side of the newspaper. Strangely, all I could see was Tiger — in my arms, his tongue lolling out between his jaws, his golden eyes paling in death. "It's just too much," I said, thickly.

Marita came over and put her arms around me.

"Janice, my dear. You must look ahead now. Your mother has found her second chance at happiness, and things are going to be better for you, too. You'll see."

I shook my head. She was not a dog lover. She would think it queer that I could be grieving for both Tiger and my father.

She reached out for a tissue and handed it to me. After I had made a great ritual of wiping my eyes, she suggested, "Why not phone Greg now and ask him if he can get off next weekend?"

I sat on the bed and she handed me the phone, then tactfully left the bedroom.

Greg was home, but he did not express much enthusiasm when I repeated Marita's invitation. "It's going to be a working weekend," I explained. "We're going to replace some broken tiles on the roof. It's leaking."

"Who's 'we'?"

"All of us. That is, the usual crowd. The men are going to fix the roof. Sandy and I will feed you. Sandy's Marita's niece."

"Marita's got a job needs doing, she puts her friends to work, huh?"

"What are friends for?" I was speaking in a low voice directly into the phone, hoping Marita could not hear me from the other room. "Please try to come, Greg. It will be lots of fun."

"Yeah, I'll bet. Well, I'd like to see this place you're so hooked on." He paused, and I waited. "I'll see if I can get one of the guys to switch weekends with me. See you tomorrow night?"

"Okay." He was not panting to go, but I had

to be satisfied. I couldn't understand why he didn't like Marita.

Greg managed the trade with his friend and Friday after work we drove down in my car, which was in better condition than Greg's beat-up Chevvy.

We drove with the windows rolled down, our hair tossed by the wind. On the radio a group was singing some catchy choruses that all ended with "I can't get enough of this," and it expressed just the way I was feeling. The third time they sang it, Greg's gleaming eyes met mine and we sang the refrain together.

We came up to the great gates of the rancho just as the sun was going down behind the coast range. They had been left open for us, and Casa de las Tres Hermanas rose at the end of the drive in impressive layers of tile-roofed wings ascending the slight slope and topped by the bell tower. In the sun's low rays the white-washed walls were splashed with gold and the few windows behind their iron bars blazed with golden fire.

Greg was driving and he involuntarily pressed down on the brakes. "Wow!"

We drank in the sight as we slowly wound up the drive through the ragged eucalyptus trees. I was glad Greg was seeing the Casa at its best.

Tony and Marita were just getting out of Tony's car when we reached the curve of the drive before the entry arch. Rick had come out to greet them, wearing dark slacks and one of those loose-sleeved white shirts that beautifully underlined his Spanish good looks.

"Paul's the chef tonight," we heard him say as Greg turned off the motor. "He's in the kitchen whipping up his gazpacho and he's got Sandy tearing lettuce for a salad. I don't suppose you brought any wine?"

"I thought you said there was a wine cellar," I called teasingly.

He looked over at us and grinned. "Hi, Janice. I didn't say there was any wine in it, did I?"

Greg was unfolding his long length from behind the steering wheel. "Rick, this is my friend, Greg Baxter."

"Rick Carrasco," he said, offering his hand as Greg came around the car. His almond-shaped eyes were slitted, lazily measuring Greg who was as tall as he was and broader in the shoulders. "Welcome to La Casa de las Tres Hermanas."

I heard the arrogant pride of possession in Rick's voice, and saw Greg's reaction to it. I hoped Greg's dislike was not as obvious to Rick and Marita.

A little later we joined Sandy and Jerry in the kitchen. Greg liked them better, I could tell. Marita's lawyer friend, Weldon, came bringing the Croft sisters, and to them Greg was respectful, with little to say. Then Paul wandered in with his guitar slung casually over his shoulder and Greg brightened. He had found someone to talk to, and he and Paul sat in a corner with their heads together, strumming chords and comparing instruments until everything else was ready and it was time to serve Paul's chilled soup, along with crusty French bread and an assortment of cheeses.

"Greg's cute," Sandy whispered as she passed me with her filled tray.

"He likes you and Jerry," I whispered back.

After we ate, Paul played Spanish songs, some mournful, some lively. I could tell Greg was enjoying himself. Rick and Sandy danced to one of the livelier tunes. Then one of the Croft sisters brought out an embroidered shawl she had picked up at an auction. "For you, Marita," she said, and flung it over Marita's shoulders.

With a lilting laugh, Marita slid the scarlet silk down and tied it around her hips. Her arms akimbo, she whirled around the kitchen. Rick arched his back and followed her, heels tapping. Sandy clapped to the rhythm of the music Paul struck up. I saw Greg's eyes widen, and wondered what he was thinking as another typical night at Casa de las Tres Hermanas was under way.

Marita was at once more fiery and more skilled than Sandy and her passionate single-mindedness in the dance seemed to inspire Rick. They danced with a curious intensity as if mesmerized by each other, and yet . . . almost as if they were adversaries.

Again I found myself comparing Rick's movements to the balletlike postures of a bullfighter. Something I had read flashed into my mind — someone had called the matador's performance "a dance with death." I did not know why, but I shivered.

CHAPTER
7

SOMEONE was scrambling around on the roof. There was a bump and a softly explosive yell, followed by a long slithering sound. Someone was sliding down to the miniature balcony jutting out from my window over the court below. My heart jumped and began beating a rapid tattoo. Someone was trying to get into my room!

"Grab him!" Tony's shout came as clearly through my open window as if he had been in my bedroom.

I was not dreaming! The sounds on the roof were real.

"Gotcha," Greg grunted.

"Thanks, kid," Paul's voice said, with a rueful note.

I opened my eyes to broad daylight.

"For heaven's sake take off your shoes, Paul. Go down and ask Marita to give you a pair of my sneakers." It was Rick. "Look, I've marked with chalk all the broken tiles I could find—"

My pumping heart slowed in relief. They were

already starting work on the roof. That was what had wakened me. I rolled out of bed and took a hasty shower.

When I walked into the kitchen Sandy was beating eggs and Marita was frying bacon. "Here's sleepyhead," she teased, "just in time to tell the men breakfast is ready."

I went out on the kitchen terrace and saw several pallets stacked with curved red tiles that had been invisible last night. A stooped man in a battered black hat was cutting the metal strapping with a tool. This must be "old Carlos" who had rung the bell last weekend, scaring us out of our wits.

"Good morning."

He lifted his head — shy eyes in a face as brown and wrinkled as a dried apricot — and muttered something that sounded like "señorita." He was older than the hills. I wondered how much English he understood.

A shiny aluminum extension ladder leaned against the overhanging eave. There were five men walking around up on the roof. No wonder they had awakened me.

"Breakfast," I called.

"Hark, the lark!" Rick said. He came swiftly down the ladder, threw a companionable arm across my shoulders and swept me back into the kitchen with him. I glanced back in time to see storm clouds in Greg's face. It warmed me to know he was bothered, seeing Rick put an arm around me. I drew away, but not too fast.

We served ourselves from the tile stove and

carried our trays outside. Sandy took a tray to Carlos, who nodded his head in thanks.

The men ate swiftly with little conversation, except for Greg, who determinedly questioned Rick.

"Are you in college?"

"Just finished two years at San Jose State."

"What's your major?"

"Liberal arts."

"That's pretty general, isn't it? What do you plan to do?"

"Run the rancho," Rick said, rather condescendingly, and popped a triangle of toast in his mouth.

"Lord of the manor," Jerry muttered.

I saw the faint grin Greg gave Jerry before he said, sounding sincerely confused, "But what do you grow here, Rick? Besides eucalyptus trees and monkey mimulus, I mean?"

I was intrigued. California flora was still new to me. Besides, I knew Greg was baiting Rick and thought I would head it off. "Why is it called monkey mimulus?"

"Because the flowers have a monkey-face," Marita told me.

"Money trees," Rick said.

"Pardon?"

Rick laughed. "I'm going to grow money trees."

Greg's eyes narrowed, but he still played dumb. "Just how do you do that? Want to share your secret?"

"We may open the Casa to tourists," Rick

said, and added, carelessly, "After it's brightened up, of course."

"Of course," Jerry murmured, and Sandy shot him a peculiar glance. A warning?

Marita jumped up. "Time!" she said, brightly.

The men climbed up on the roof again, moving gingerly over the slippery tiles. The sun was already hot and they had pulled off their shirts. Clothes do make a difference, I thought, amused.

Paul was frankly pudgy. He took the baked clay tiles Sandy and I passed up the ladder and passed them to Jerry, skinny, wiry, and light on his feet, who distributed them to the other three.

I looked at Tony, solid, and strong, and surprisingly capable at what must be unfamiliar work, and thought that his clothes did not do him justice. How could my mother fall in love with Kelly when her boss was a man like that?

Rick and Greg were two sides of a coin, one so dark, the other so fair. Rick, as tall as Greg but narrower in the shoulders, was brown and completely hairless, with the suppleness of a sleek cat. But I knew I would always carry the memory of Greg like a picture in an album, shirtless and tanned, standing on the red-tiled roof with the breeze lifting his fair hair as he gazed over the trees toward the mountains.

Marita was everywhere in her beautifully cut jeans, urging us on with her limitless enthusiasm, directing operations all along the assembly line she had set up, egging us on, good-humoredly, sometimes with acid humor. As the sun climbed higher, she went into the kitchen and came out with cool cans of beer which we passed up to the men, who sat cross-legged on the tiles to drink them.

Just before noon, the Croft sisters came bringing a fat package of sliced salami and spelled us passing up tiles while Sandy and I made sandwiches. The men came down and we all sat on the terrace to eat.

To my annoyance Rick sat on the stones at my feet, quite as if I hadn't brought Greg down for the weekend. Greg watched us, rather glumly. Before we'd finished eating they got into an argument about Rick's theories on what he called "natural" gardening.

"I never trim anything," he told Greg, in his superior way. "I simply let nature take its course. After all, nature knows best."

"Not always," Greg snorted. "In nature it's the survival of the strongest. In a dry year like the winter just past, you could lose some of your trees. One of those tall eucalyptus trees could fall across your roof and smash your new tiles."

"You practice my theory in your park, don't you?" Rick argued. "You have to let nature have her way. Isn't that the whole idea of a park?"

"Don't you believe it!" Greg retorted. "If we left the brushing out to nature, she'd do it with forest fires."

"What Rick is saying," Tony told Greg, with his easy, relaxed humor, "is that he can't afford gardeners."

71

Greg laughed with the others, and presently we rose to go back to work. But the tension between him and Rick was still there.

That evening we were all tired but exhilarated and self-congratulatory as we parted to go to our rooms and clean up. After our showers, we were too relaxed to do much but sprawl around the burning eucalyptus logs in the kitchen fireplace.

"No dancing tonight," Sandy groaned.

"No gourmet food," Marita told us.

Jerry stood up. "I'll go get some pizzas, Marita. Want to come along, Sandy?"

Sandy got up immediately.

I had an impulse to say, "Let's go with them, Greg," when Marita spoke drily. "Don't be all night. We're hungry." I realized then that Jerry and Sandy wanted to be alone.

But they were not gone long, and when we had eaten the pizzas they brought back, we were all ready to call it a day.

Sunday morning we finished the roof, and cheered ourselves. Greg wanted to get home early and we were the first to leave the Casa.

I settled back against the car seat with a happy sigh. "A great weekend, wasn't it?"

"Yeah," Greg said, "bizarre."

I stiffened. "I thought you were having fun, Greg."

"If you can call working our butts off all weekend fun. Why do they all do it? Can't they see Marita is using them?"

I was offended. "They seem to enjoy it."

"Yeah."

I watched the road unwinding ahead of us and said nothing. After all, Greg had not been shown through the Casa.

Presently he said, "It's a mess, isn't it? My chief ranger would have a fit if he saw the grounds. He'd rate the fire hazard extreme."

I was stunned. Was that all Greg saw?

"It's going to be a blazing summer, too. We're going into the dry season without enough rainfall. Do you know we've already had five 'extreme hazard' days posted on our board in the park, and it's not even July? If I were Marita I'd be worrying about that instead of the roof."

I was miserably silent, disappointed that he could not share my pleasure in the Casa. It seemed to me like another world, one that the hum of the unseen highway beyond the iron gates could not penetrate. Its charm was that of stepping back into the past, not as it was lived in the affluent days of Casa de las Tres Hermanas when there must have been dozens of servants and gardeners, but into a faded dream of the past, its glamour tarnished, its days lazy and as unreal as a two A.M. movie.

Greg didn't seem to notice my silence. "Why do they bother?" he mused. "Those tiles are so old they're crumbling. I wouldn't be surprised to find we did as much damage walking on them as we repaired."

I found my voice. "Greg, you haven't really seen the Casa yet. There are tennis courts —"

"I saw them. The slabs are all cracked and mossy."

"The boarded-up wings are filled with the most fabulous treasures from their Spanish heritage. Marita and Rick and Sandy and their friends are all devoted to preserving them. Marita is sacrificing a lot to save the Casa. She couldn't do it alone, and her friends are glad to help."

"Uh-huh. But what has she got against Jerry? I happen to think he's a regular guy and he's certainly helping out. Yet she was always putting him down."

I laughed. "Oh, she says she wants a millionaire for Sandy, someone who can afford to renovate the Casa."

"Yecch. Then why is she always inviting you down for Pretty Boy?"

"She *doesn't*."

"The way Marita dotes on him she must think he rates at least a millionairess."

"Don't be gross!" I snapped. "It's a joke, Greg. It was Marita who suggested I bring you down. You're making me sorry I did."

"I'm not trying to insult you, Janice. But I've got a funny feeling about that bunch. I can't put my finger on it, but there's something odd going on."

"That's the most ridiculous alibi for being jealous I have ever heard."

"I'm not jealous!" He shrugged, then grinned at me. "Well, not much. But since Marita is using all her friends, I can't help wondering just what use she has for you."

I was suddenly fighting tears. I stared through them at the blurred road and said between clenched jaws, "I would rather be used than thought useless!"

"I didn't say that!" he shouted. Then his ears got very red, and his jaws tightened. "What I meant was — what's she planning? You don't belong in that crowd, Janice. Marita must be nearly as old as your mother."

"Leave my mother out of this!"

"Okay, oka-a-ay!" His foot was suddenly heavy on the accelerator.

We rode the rest of the way in silence and when he stopped before Marita's apartment building, I opened the door and grabbed my suitcase before he could get out to help me.

"I'll call you —" Greg began.

"If you think I'm so useless, don't bother." I slammed the car door and ran. Behind me I heard him gun the motor and roar off.

Marita's telephone was ringing when I unlocked the door. I dropped my suitcase and ran to answer it. When I heard my mother's voice, I began to cry.

"Janice, I'm so sorry about Tiger, but please don't cry. I want to hear all about it and why you are staying with Marita. Mrs. Crowder is quite upset about your leaving. Janice, how can you tell me about it when you are crying, baby?"

That did it. I am not her baby. "Mrs. Crowder

couldn't stand Tiger barking in the night. She wouldn't believe I had a prowler. So she poisoned him."

"Janice, you can't really believe that Mrs. Crowder would do that?"

"That's what the vet said."

"Not that Mrs. Crowder poisoned him, surely."

"Who else?"

"I don't know. I can't imagine anyone being so horrible and certainly not the Crowders. They would simply ask us to leave, if Tiger bothered them that much. Are you happy with Marita? It is so good of her to take you in. I feel better knowing you are there instead of by yourself, even though the Crowders were keeping a close eye on you for me."

"Were they ever!" I said, bitterly. "The night the prowler came, Mrs. Crowder asked me if I was entertaining Greg in my room."

"Were you?" It was Kelly's teasing voice.

"Where did you come from?" I asked, resentfully.

"Sorry. Your mother should have told you she was handing me the phone."

"Well said, Red."

He laughed. "Listen, Jan."

I stiffened.

"Don't judge Mrs. Crowder too hastily. She could be a busybody but she's not the type that sneaks around poisoning dogs."

"Who is?"

"You may have a point there. All I'm saying

76

is don't be hasty. Reserve judgement, okay? And what's this about a prowler, anyway?"

"Thanks for trying, Red. Will you put my mother back on, please?"

"Did you have a prowler, Janice?" my mother asked.

"I wasn't going to tell you because you would worry. But it didn't worry the Crowders. Anyway, Tiger scared him off." My throat tightened again.

"Well, you're with Marita now, thank heaven. But about the Crowders — Kelly's advice is good, Janice," my mother said, gently.

"Yeah," I said. "Are you calling from Mexico?"

"Yes." She gave me the name of their hotel. "We are on a marvelous little beach not far from Ensenada. It's heavenly quiet and so beautiful! Sometime I'd like you to see it."

"Yeah, sometime."

"We'll stay here now, until Kelly has to come back to work."

Her voice had changed. She sounded so deliciously happy that I was nauseated. I didn't tell her I had quarreled with Greg.

CHAPTER

8

TONY Kapel had to go to Sacramento to confer with state engineers about a construction project. He and Marita worked late several nights preparing his material, so I had too much time alone. I was still angry with Greg, waiting for his apology. It didn't help to receive a postcard with scrawled wish-you-were-here messages from both Kelly and my mother, and a picture of sand so white and water so blue they didn't look real.

Late Thursday evening Tony telephoned Marita from Sacramento to say he was staying over for more meetings on Monday. Marita just assumed I would go to Casa de las Tres Hermanas with her. Greg had not called and I thought, all right, let him call and find me gone.

But it was very different from my other weekends at the Casa. Perhaps the things Greg said had opened my eyes. Or maybe it was because we arrived in the middle of a crisis.

No one came out to greet us, but a distraught

Sandy with muddy jeans and tangled hair met us just inside the front door. She didn't say hello; she was not even smiling. She just ran her hands up her temples through her fair hair and said, "Everybody's up in the canyon but Weldon. He's on the phone, trying to prevent a lawsuit."

"A lawsuit?" Marita said, sharply, setting down her overnight case.

"We're sure Carlos did it. He must have used dynamite. Where do you suppose he got it? Weldon says they will want to know. Don't flush your john," Sandy warned, distractedly.

Marita turned pale. "He didn't blast the water line!"

Sandy nodded. "The water company sent inspectors out and Carlos ordered them off with a shotgun."

White-faced, eyes black with fury, Marita exploded in harsh Spanish. I didn't understand a word but there was no mistaking its profanity.

When Marita paused for breath, Sandy said, "Weldon thinks if we can fix it right away there may not be trouble."

"What is it, a water district line?" I asked, timidly.

Marita looked at me with blank eyes that slowly changed as if she were just remembering me. She drew a deep breath. "It's the water for the subdivision," she said, in a barely controlled voice. "We gave them an easement over our property. Carlos has forgotten — there was a big battle over water rights when he was a young vaquero here. He lives in the past."

"Weldon says if we blame it on Carlos they may commit him."

"Let them try it!" Marita blazed at Sandy. She began spitting Spanish again but the color was returning to her face.

I was touched by her arrogant defense of the old man and when she finished in an exhausted way, "Oh, God, where is the money coming from?" I felt deeply sorry for her.

But in the next moment she said, "Where is Carlos now?"

"Sedated." Rick had come in from the direction of the kitchen. "The doctor gave him something." Rick's clothes were muddy, too.

"Poor chicks, you've had a rough time, haven't you?" Marita was girding herself for battle now. The defiant blaze in her eyes had lowered to a steady glow, and the movements of her thin body had an alert tension.

"Marita, dear!" Weldon was coming through the dining gallery toward us. It was the first time I had seen him in anything but corduroys and a sweater; his shoes were muddy, but in his coat and tie, he looked very much the successful young lawyer. I had never before noticed how nice his eyes were, a soft and velvety brown.

"Thank you for coming, Weldon. How bad is it?"

"If we can fix the line promptly I think you can avoid trouble. I've promised them we will furnish the labor if they will deliver the replacement pipe. They will send a foreman with the tools."

"And I will have to pay him time-and-a-half," Marita said, sharply. I had never seen her look like this — almost haggard, with two deep lines beside her mouth and her eyes desperate. I realized for the first time how really deep was her emotional commitment to Casa de las Tres Hermanas.

"Rick and I have ordered the necessary materials," Weldon said, calmly. "Paul and Jerry will come after work to help us. We may have to work through the night, but if we can restore service before morning I don't think they will sue."

Some of her tension seemed to drain away. "What would I do without you, Weldon?"

He grinned, happily. "Hang by your thumbs, probably." In an intuitive flash, I knew that Weldon would do anything Marita asked of him. That smart young lawyer was in love.

"I'm going up to change." Marita ran up the stairs.

"It happened while Rick and I were at work," Sandy told me, running her hands up into her hair again.

"Oh, Sandy, have you got a job?"

"For the summer. In a dress shop. Tell you about it later." She was pale and she talked jerkily. "Carlos was raving when we got home; we couldn't get any sense from him. I called

Doctor Jarman and he came and gave Carlos a shot. Then the water district called and said the subdivision had been without water for two hours and that Carlos had ordered their inspector off with a shotgun. Wild!"

"Carlos has a gun?" I was feeling less safe every minute, wishing I had stayed in Santa Teresa.

"It's an old piece," Rick said, shrugging. "I don't even know if it will fire. He must have stumbled over the water line and thought someone was stealing our water."

Sandy said, "He's just not with it half the time. We can't imagine where he got the dynamite. We've been frantic. Weldon's been on the phone for an hour, negotiating."

"Here come the others now." Rick opened the front door, and I heard the crunch of automobile tires on the gravel of the drive.

Marita was back, running silently on sneakered feet. She had put on jeans and a shirt and carried a sweater. Her face had lost its desperation and was now intent and purposeful. Buoyed by the support of her friends, she was already enjoying the challenge.

Nothing had been prepared for dinner. All the men, Marita with them in her fitted jeans, went up the trail that wound up the canyon to where the break in the line occurred. Sandy and I stayed behind to make sandwiches and a gallon of coffee.

When we climbed up through the monkey mimulus and live oak with our hampers, carrying flashlights because the sky was already gray with dusk, we found to my astonishment an air of carnival at the work site. Marita, who had apparently charmed the water district foreman into bemused wonder, was tacitly in charge just as she had been on the day when the roof was repaired. Gone was her desperate fury. She radiated energy and enthusiasm. There was the same camaraderie among the men, as though they were enjoying labor to which they were unaccustomed.

In spite of the damp night air, Rick and Jerry were shirtless, their bodies glowing in the kerosene light. I thought of Greg and what he would say when I told him everyone was willing to work all night. He would never believe it was like a picnic.

Sandy and I stayed to eat sandwiches and drink coffee with them, then we went back down the dark trail to make more.

That was the story of our night. We must have made gallons of coffee and umpteen trips carrying them with flashlights to light our way up the narrow trail. At midnight we made more sandwiches.

Marita was doing what she did best, charming all of us into working as if it were play. Her infectious enthusiasm drove us all.

But for me it was not the same. Greg's voice kept repeating in my memory, "She uses her friends."

I knew a little more about these people now. I had guessed Weldon was in love with Marita. I could not detect any difference in her expression when she turned to Paul but, watching Paul, I became convinced that he was in love with her, too. Perhaps his was a secret, hopeless love. But if I could detect it, surely Marita knew?

And what about Tony Kapel?

Actually, she seemed fonder of Rick than she was of any one of the three men. I watched her, wondering how she did it. She turned on that charismatic charm; actually, she sort of flirted with all of them, even Rick. She kept them dangling. Using them.

Toward morning Rick came down the trail to telephone the water company. I was alone in the kitchen, half-asleep over the sink, washing a few dishes. Sandy, exhausted by the wild events of the day and its demands on her, had gone up to her room to take a nap after making me promise to call her in an hour.

Rick was arranging with the water district's service department to have the inspector out as soon as he came on duty in the morning. He hung the phone back on the wall and walked over to the sink and put his arms around me. Before I could make a protest, he had lifted me off my feet and set me down in a chair. Then he quickly went back to the sink and took over my task. He was like Marita, still blazing with energy although the clock had struck four. Where did all that energy come from?

"You're effective in the kitchen," I said, watching his graceful hands rinse and sort the dishes in a quick, well-organized way.

"I've had to be. If we couldn't maintain the Casa ourselves it would have gone up for auction long ago."

"I've wondered how Marita manages. It's you and Sandy who manage, isn't it?"

"When my mother died and Marita — she'd just been divorced — came back to California to take care of us, there wasn't enough money for a housekeeper, so Marita sat down and analyzed the work, then divided it up between the three of us."

I laughed. "That sounds like her. How old were you and Sandy then?"

"About ten and twelve. Hungry for responsibility. And as determined as Marita to stay here, in spite of inheritance taxes and all that."

"But it was Casa de las Tres Hermanas pulling her back," I said, thinking out loud, almost asleep, "not just the needs of two orphans."

"Oh, we were not orphans," Rick said, casually. "Our father was killed later in a gambling quarrel in Tijuana. He had deserted us years before that."

"Oh," I said, inadequately. "Was he Spanish, too?"

"With a name like Nicholas Sabin?" Rick said, slanting an amused but oddly watchful look at me. "Same as mine," he added, offhand.

"Is that what the Rick is for? I thought it must be Ricardo." I was desperately trying to keep my eyes open, because this was interesting.

"Do you like Ricardo better? Maybe I'll change my name. Marita made us use Carrasco instead of Sabin because the Carrascos must not be allowed to die out."

He lifted his dripping hands and turned his dark eyes on me. He was so incongruously handsome! It crossed my mind that few men, or women either, could wash dishes with such style.

"How does it sound? 'Señora Ricardo Sabin y Carrasco.'" He rolled the r's out in beautiful trills. "It's the Spanish way, you know, to tack on the maternal name."

I blinked, not understanding until he added, "You know what 'señora' means, don't you?" He laughed at me. "I'm asking you to marry me, Janice."

My eyes flew wide open. "Me . . . get married?"

"Why don't we do it now? Just get in the car and go?" The black glitter coming from beneath his lashes revealed the same driving force that I felt sometimes in Marita — like a strong north wind that blew everything before its desire. "We might as well make a night of it, don't you think?"

Was I dreaming this? "Rick, you're crazy!"

In a swift change the glitter in his eyes became dangerous as he warned, "Don't ever call me crazy!"

"I — I didn't mean —" I stuttered. What was with this guy? I was glad when Sandy walked in, interrupting us. Rick banged the kitchen door as he went out and we heard him running along the house toward the trail.

"Go take a nap," Sandy ordered, yawning. "I can carry on now."

"I'm not sleepy." I wasn't, now. I got up, turning away from her to conceal my face which must be reflecting the confused thoughts running through my head. A proposal of marriage! How did I handle this?

While we made more coffee and cut up some crusty bread, Sandy and I talked about the Casa. She was more detached about the old ruin than Marita was, and she told me more about the Carrascos who were their ancestors.

"The first Carrasco we know anything about was a Spanish noble who came up from Mexico as an aide to the governor of California and was given a land grant of two hundred and fifty thousand acres." .

"Wow!"

"Yeah, wow," she said, smiling. "That was only a few years before the American settlers here raised their bear flag of rebellion."

"Did the United States confiscate his land?"

"No. But he fell on hard times and sold some of it. Then when he died it was divided among his sons, who sold some more. My great-grandfather built this house. As you can see he was still very wealthy, a land baron. He had twenty servants and I don't know how many vaqueros to herd his cattle.

"But the Carrascos have gone downhill ever since his day. The name disappeared long ago, since the Carrascos had daughters, not sons.

The *tres hermanas* were the last Carrasco women. It's a miracle the house and the few remaining acres are still in the family." Her lips quirked in a half smile. "Probably won't be much longer."

"I think your Carrasco blood must be thinner," I said, lazily.

"Why?" she asked, amused.

"You don't have Marita's drive to save the Casa, do you? And I can't imagine you in a temper."

"You haven't seen anything yet!" Sandy retorted, a slight edge to her voice.

I had not meant to invite criticism of Marita, nor did I want to. But I felt a vague alarm. "Why do you say that?"

"Marita has convinced Rick he is God's gift to women," she told me, with her little grin. "A rejection was good for him, but don't expect him to take it gracefully."

I knew then that she had overheard him. "Sandy, I'm just sixteen!"

"Uh-huh."

What alarmed me most was the intimation that she had taken Rick's strange, insensitive proposal seriously. How could she?

"You know, I wouldn't be sorry to leave the Casa," she remarked presently, in a musing tone. And then, before I could ask her if she were going to marry Jerry, she added more briskly, "But of course, Marita never will."

"In a way I admire her for her commitment," I said. I had been thinking about it quite a lot since my quarrel with Greg. "I think it is Marita's unshakable enthusiasm that draws us all to her. You know, Sandy, there are few people who have a strong commitment to an ideal, so that when we meet it, the force of it acts on us like a magnet. I think that's true of Marita."

"You could be right." Sandy yawned again.

Jerry came in with the thermos jug. "The guys want more coffee and sandwiches."

We found the men just finishing the repairs and getting ready to test the system. The repaired section held when the water was turned back on, and we all went to bed, exhausted. Someone — probably Rick — must have wakened to take the inspector up the canyon, but I slept until after noon Saturday.

That evening Weldon and Jerry came back with a couple of large pizzas, and Paul came bringing his guitar. We sat around, listening to the men tease each other about their ineptness with a shovel and a wrench, as Paul played his sad Spanish folksongs, but we were all still exhausted. It was really a dreadful parody of our other good times. I saw how much Tony Kapel had added to the pattern of our fun. Besides being charming, he had added a mysterious element of stability that I now perceived was lacking. And I missed Greg terribly.

We were in a small sitting room across the entry from the living room, where Marita had suggested we take our coffee because there were sofas and more comfortable chairs. I volunteered to refill the coffee pot and Rick got lazily to his feet, offering to help me.

In the kitchen he put his arms loosely around me and said, in a low conspiratorial voice, "When you go upstairs, pack your bag. I'll meet you downstairs at midnight. We can drive across the Tehachapi pass and be in Las Vegas by morning."

Sandy was so right. Rick would not take rejection gracefully. He would not take it, period. I tried to be more diplomatic this time.

"Rick, you can't be serious. I'm not even thinking about marriage yet. Didn't Marita tell you? Rick, I'm sixteen!"

"You can pass for eighteen."

"My mother would have it annulled, immediately. Besides, I don't want to get married."

Rick grinned wolfishly. "You just think you don't."

I had my back to the counter and he was facing me. I tried to slip away but he leaned forward and rested his weight on the table with one arm on each side of me. Without touching me, he was effectively barring my escape.

"Please, Rick," I begged. "You will make it impossible for me to come back here."

Dismay showed in his face. "Janice, don't say that!"

"Then forget eloping. Just forget it!"

"Forget it!" he repeated, bitterly. But I thought I saw a fleeting calculation in his eyes before he took me in his arms. It stunned me.

Then I was furious, as his hard grasp held my arms imprisoned, and his lips found my cheek, my chin, my hair, and finally my lips. His kiss was too intimate, too demanding. Instead of exciting me, which I realized he was deliberately trying to do, it turned me off.

I twisted away from him, furious. "Get your hands off me, Rick! You're behaving like a sophomore on his first date!"

His grasp tightened cruelly. Too late I realized that I had given the unforgivable insult. I tried to soften it. "Don't you know you can't force —"

"Don't you know that you can't refuse?" he mocked me.

"My, what a tender scene!" Marita said gaily, from the doorway. Behind her Paul began humming a teasing Spanish love song. "Don't let us interrupt. Paul decided we should have some sherry, but perhaps we should make it champagne?"

Rick's arms had slackened and I broke away. Crying "Oh, leave me alone!" I turned and ran, down the long dining gallery, through the living room. Past the staring others in the little sitting room and up the wide stairs. Along the corridor, finally, to my room.

When someone knocked at my door a little later, I was in bed with all the lights out, pretending to be asleep. I was sure it was Rick at my door. I knew now that I did not even like him very well. And I had behaved so awkwardly. I thought of Marita dangling her three suitors, all so eager to help her, and told myself she must be laughing at me. She would have handled it tactfully, without losing her temper.

But Greg never would have pushed like that. If Greg had been here, none of it would have happened. The whole weekend was a mistake, I thought, dismally, wondering if I would ever be able to come back to Casa de las Tres Hermanas. In spite of Rick I had enjoyed my weekends here.

He was still outside my door. Marita must have come after him, for I heard her say quite clearly, "Leave her alone, Rick."

"She'll let me in. I think I should talk to her." I am sure they thought I could not hear what they were saying through the Casa's thick doors, for Marita said, sharply, "You fool! When did you ever think? I do the thinking!"

"Cool it, Mar. I've done nothing I can't mend."

Arrogant, as always. But I had been surprised at Marita's sharp tone, to Rick whom she adored.

Their voices had dropped lower and I could not distinguish what they said, until I heard Marita's harsh penetrating whisper: "— I could kill you!"

"— except that you need me." I could hear in Rick's confident voice the superior smile that must be on his lips. "How far can you go without me?"

I don't know what Marita said then, but I heard Rick run back down the stairs and a moment later the front door slammed. A car started up and roared down the drive. I knew it was Rick, going away angry.

Evidently, Marita had given him a piece of her mind, and not only for trying to kiss me. There was more to their quarrel than that, I thought uneasily. But I did not see then what it was.

CHAPTER
9

THE nightmare began as it had always begun, with schools of silvery fish in black water, moving in shifting patterns, changing color like leaves turning in the breeze. Beautiful, but terrifyingly sinister for I knew what was coming.

And then they were there, the menacing dark shapes throwing their shadows over the darting fish, rolling and turning above them, scattering them in a frantic scramble. And I was one of the fish, darting this way and that in terror, trying to escape, but trapped.

I wakened with a cry and lay listening to the loud thudding of my heart. It was still dark and very quiet. I missed the thump of Tiger's tail beside my bed. For a moment I lay thinking of my dog, missing him.

Then my thoughts shifted to that embarrassing quarrel with Rick last night and I didn't feel any better. It certainly was not what I would call cool to make a scene with a houseful of guests listening in. I could have throttled

Rick for forcing me to do something so gauche as run upstairs to my room, and then following me to pound on my door!

Beneath my resentment I was confused and worried. What was I missing in all this? Something important. Because it just didn't make sense. I do the thinking, Marita had said. About what, exactly?

I turned restlessly in bed. I was used to getting up at dawn and running out on the trail with Tiger. Well, I could run by myself, couldn't I? Run some of the doubts and questions out of my mind? Because I just couldn't stay in bed any longer.

The living room was in deep shadow, with a brilliant square of light falling from the kitchen door into the dining gallery beyond it. As I passed, I caught the glow of a cigarette and its reflection in one of the dark, heavily barred front windows. For a moment I froze. Then I marched on, through the entry hall, and let myself out the front door.

I ran across the tiled arcade and down the drive, ran like the wind, breathing in the sharp air, the aroma that would always take me back to this drive in the moonlight with the naked trunks of the gum trees gleaming ghostly white between their tatters of peeling bark, and conjured up an image of Greg running lightly and easily beside me.

At the locked iron gates I circled and ran, more slowly now, back to the house. I was breathing fast but glowing with energy when I opened the door and stopped in the archway to the living room.

Marita said, calmly, "Good morning, Janice." She was in a short, dark kimono with her bare feet thrust into scuffs. She was still looking out across the loggia to the dark tangle of shrubs beyond it, thoughtfully smoking.

"Aren't you up early?"

"A little," she said, smiling slightly. "I was just trying to decide whether to go back to bed, or have a cup of coffee. Want some?"

When I hesitated she said, "You don't have to worry about running into Rick this morning. He phoned me from San Jose last night. He's up there with a college friend."

"Oh," I said. And then, feeling awkward, "Marita, I'm sorry I lost my cool."

Again she gave me that rather absent little smile.

I followed her into the kitchen. She took down two pottery mugs and filled them from the pot on the tile stove. The coffee smelled strong and fresh. She handed me a mug, and took hers to the oak work table. I sat across from her and for a few minutes we drank the hot liquid in silence.

Presently Marita said, in a carefully flat voice, "What did Rick do wrong?"

Wrong? "Marita, did you know Rick was asking me to elope?"

"So?"

I stared at her.

She shook her hair back, with a rueful look. "How could any woman resist him?"

"Marita, I'm only sixteen!"

"My grandmother was married when she was fifteen."

"What has your grandmother to do with me?" I was becoming angry all over again.

Marita's faint smile said, "Oh, how little you know!" Just like my mother, I thought, resenting her. It was the first time I had felt any age barrier with Marita. And then I thought, no, she is not at all like my mother. My mother would have been furious at Rick.

"You're a lucky girl, you know. Rick really wants to marry you. And he is old enough to know what he wants." She sipped her coffee. "Old enough to marry."

"Rick old enough? After the way he behaved last night?"

"He loves you, Janice."

"But I don't want to be married!" I cried. She gave me that superior smile again, so I added, "Someday, maybe, but *never* to Rick."

I thought maybe I would like to marry Greg someday. But I had sent him away, I thought, forlornly. He was going off to college in the fall, and who knew what would happen?

Marita was looking at me with a strange flat expression and too late I thought, Oh, Janice, when will you learn to think before you speak? I knew that in Marita's world the sun and the moon and all the stars shone only for Rick.

"Scratch that, Marita. I guess I'm still angry at Rick. I don't like being pushed."

"It's all right," she said. But I knew it wasn't. I had offended her — and she had been so good to me.

She rose and stretched her arms above her head. "It's going to be another fine day. What do you say we get Sandy up and go for a hike to loosen up the aching muscles?"

There was no way I could undo what I had done.

We left after breakfast, climbing the hill back of the Casa instead of taking the canyon trail so familiar since last night. For the first time I saw where Carlos, the old vaquero lived. He stood in the door of his stable-cottage, his bald head and wrinkled face brown as a nut, apparently none the worse for his adventures and sedation. As he waved to us, shouting a Spanish phrase, I wondered if he even remembered what he had done. Marita shouted back in Spanish.

We climbed to ground high enough that we could look down into the Casa itself. I picked out the inner court with the dead fountain and the tubbed citrus trees that my bedroom overlooked. Behind it and nearer us was the larger court, also completely enclosed, that I had seen from the bell tower. A tiny triangle of blue tile identified the forlorn swimming pool where the dead bird lay half-buried in eucalyptus leaves. There were other smaller courts whose existence I had not guessed, suggesting a veritable maze of corridors and galleries in the unused portion of the house.

I had a curious fancy, looking down on it. It was as if my world lurched and gave a quarter-turn and, as it tilted, a lid slid open, exposing dark, dusty caverns beneath the surface of the bright and casual life I had enjoyed at Casa de las Tres Hermanas. In a moment the lid closed and my sense of looking into unfathomable depths disappeared, but my world did not completely right itself. Now everything was slightly off-key.

Sandy had been rather quiet during the climb, but as we fell behind Marita plunging back down toward the house, she murmured, "Don't be stampeded, Janice. You've got plenty of time."

"Don't worry, Sandy." I smiled at her with genuine liking and she returned my smile. But I knew that I would not return to Casa de las Tres Hermanas, and the thought saddened me.

It might be awkward staying with Marita until my mother and Kelly came home, now that I had offended her. I could kill you, she had told Rick. That's how badly she had wanted me to say yes. I couldn't believe it! I would never feel easy with her again.

We came back down much faster than we had climbed and after a shower and a bite of lunch Marita and I packed our overnight cases to return to Santa Teresa. I hugged Sandy. Would I ever see her again?

It was windy and little twists of dust whirled

across the road. The mountains were obscured by haze and the air smelled smoky. "More forest fires," Marita said. "Some of this annoying dust is soot. The radio this morning said there are several new blazes in the Santa Cruz Mountains." She flicked on her fog lights as we entered another twister of black particles. "I hope the weather is better next weekend."

"I've been thinking," I said, in a false, apologetic voice that annoyed me, "that I'd better stay home next weekend. I need to spend some time mending and" — I forced a laugh. — "mending and laundering, you know. I've been going so much, letting things slide . . ."

"Oh, you really are frightened, aren't you? Damn Rick, anyway!" She was silent a moment, and I didn't know what to say.

"But that does sound like a smart idea, Janice. I should do the same thing — but I probably won't." Marita's laugh cleared the air.

I turned to her, relieved. "You have been so good to me, Marita. You know how I've loved going down to the Casa with you, don't you?"

" 'Loved?' " she asked, lightly.

"Well," I stammered. "My mother and Kelly will be back soon and I probably won't have time —"

"Oh, I'm sure we'll see you again. Sandy is very fond of you, you know. And I want to have your mother and Kelly down when they come back. I think Kelly and Tony are friends, aren't they? But about next weekend —" She hesitated. "I wasn't going to spoil Sandy's surprise, but you don't have to tell her, do you? You can act surprised."

"At what?" I asked, bewildered.

"She and Jerry are announcing their engagement next weekend. They'll want you there."

"Sandy and Jerry?" I exclaimed, delighted. "Oh, I think that's great, Marita."

"Then you'll come? I promise you Rick will behave."

I reflected only a moment. "I'll come."

Once more, I promised myself.

"Good."

And so we began the week that was to be my last with Marita. We were still friends, if not quite as easy with one another as before.

I had a strange interview with Tony Kapel after he came back from Sacramento. My desk was near my supervisor's, and I couldn't help overhearing Ms. Evans say, talking into her telephone, "Wouldn't you rather have Sharon, Mr. Kapel? . . . Yes, she does need the experience, but —" And then, "Yes, of course, Mr. Kapel."

Ms. Evans came directly to my desk so I knew she had been talking about me. "Mr. Kapel has some dictation. He asked expressly for you, Janice." She looked doubtful — I was not very skilled at shorthand.

I picked up a notebook and went down the hall to knock on Tony's door. I was pretty sure it wasn't dictation Tony wanted from me and I was curious.

"Come in, Janice."

He was alone in his office. I sat down at his desk and he dictated a couple of short memos, so slowly I could not have missed transcribing them. Then he said, "Are you rich, Janice?"

I thought he was joking. "We can eat. Why?"

"I'm serious, Janice. And I mean very rich. Like in heiress."

I almost dropped my pencil. Then I asked again, carefully, "Why?" I was still not sure he wasn't teasing me.

"Has it ever occurred to you to wonder why Marita has invited you along on her dates with me?"

I was too stunned to answer. It was too much like Greg asking, "But why you?"

"It has occurred to me," Tony said.

I sucked in my breath. "I'm sorry if I've been in the way."

"I didn't say I hadn't enjoyed it," he said, a twinkle lighting his eyes. "But it has made me wonder. Why would an attractive woman insist on dragging a girl who is both younger and prettier than she is on all her dates?" His lips quirked. "In all modesty, Janice, I can say that is something that has never before happened to this quite 'eligible bachelor.' "

I could believe it, but I was too surprised to speak.

"Am I the bait," Tony mused, "or are you? You're a very pretty girl, Janice, but you are a bit young for me."

"You *are* teasing me, aren't you, Tony?"

"No, Janice. I want you to think about it. What is Marita up to?"

I could hear Greg saying, "What use does she have for you?" Now I wondered what use she had for Tony. It had already occurred to me that Marita might have been hoping he would take Sandy away from Jerry, and I blurted out, "Sandy is going to announce her engagement to Jerry next weekend."

Tony didn't even blink. "Is she, indeed? I'm glad she has spunk enough to go with her own choice." I was pretty sure then that Marita had picked him for Sandy, and that he was aware of the way she had hoped to use him.

"Will you be going down for the party?" I asked him.

"No. I'm going to be tied up." There was a sound of finality in his tone, as if he, too, had written off our trips to the Casa.

CHAPTER

10

ALL day I thought about Tony's surprising remarks — worrying about them in the back of my mind while I copied reports and filled in government forms on the typewriter. I could not decide whether or not he had been teasing me. But by the end of the day I had made one decision. I had made up my mind to call Greg.

I was tired of waiting for him to call me, and I wanted badly to tell him that I regretted our quarrel. I thought he would be interested to hear that Sandy was planning to marry Jerry, for he liked them both.

I waited until Marita was in the shower that evening. It had never before been difficult to pick up the phone and dial Greg's number, but this time my heart was doing double-time. His young brother answered, and I heard him yell loudly, "Hey, jock, your girlfriend's on the line."

Greg's hello was a wary question.

"It's me, Greg."

"Janice!" He sounded surprised, but pleased. "Hey!"

"How are things in the wilderness?"

"It's wild, all right, but no wilderness. People are trampling each other in the campground. I hate to think what it'll be like next weekend."

I plunged ahead, in a hurry to say what I had to say before Marita emerged from the bathroom. "Speaking of weekends, the next will be my last at the Casa. I hate to admit it, but you were at least partly right about that."

"Then why are you going back next weekend?"

A logical question. That was Greg. Straight to the heart of whatever we were discussing. Nothing had changed. "Because Sandy is announcing her engagement."

"Yeah?" Skeptical, too.

"To Jerry."

"Hey, that's great!" he said, with all the warmth and sweetness that cool, logical mind of his could not conceal. I felt unreasonably happy.

"Isn't it? I'm really pleased. Can you get off, Greg?" I was sure Sandy and Jerry would want him there, too, and I didn't care much what Marita and Rick thought.

But he said, "No way. It's a holiday weekend."

"It is?"

"Remember Independence Day? The worst weekend of the summer in the park, they tell me."

Dumb me. "I guess I've been wrapped up in my own little world."

"Yeah," he drawled.

Well, I deserved that, I guess. "Jerry would be so pleased. Are you sure?"

"No way I can get off. But I could meet you at the drive-in in ten minutes. I'd sure like to see you, Janice."

"It's nine o'clock, Greg." But I wanted desperately to see him.

"Just long enough for a soda?"

"You're on."

I grabbed my car keys, scribbled a note to Marita, and was out of the apartment before she could emerge from her bath and ask what my mother would say.

Greg was standing in a parking space to hold it for me when I drove up. He climbed in my passenger seat as soon as I stopped. "Outside service, right?"

"Right."

I had the windows rolled down. The warm night air carried tantalizing odors of hamburger and fries along with the pollens of summer.

"Two ice cream sodas, one chocolate, one strawberry," Greg called to the girl who was carhopping. We turned to each other. "I've missed you, Janice."

"I've missed you, Greg."

"Don't do that — shut me out like that — again, please."

"I won't," I promised, my heart full.

His eyes shone, a blue flame in the light spilling through my window from the drive-in. He leaned forward and brushed my lips with a soft kiss, and I put my arms around him and kissed him back.

"Ya-ay, Greg, "someone said softly from a nearby car.

Greg just held me closer.

Our sodas came, and we sat touching, drawing on our straws and talking. Greg had his left arm around me, his fingers playing with my hair. "I'm glad you're not going down to that place anymore. The whole set-up is weird, including the people."

I resented that. "No, Greg. I really like everybody — except Rick. Do you know he had the brass to suggest we elope last weekend? Just leave, in the middle of the night?"

Greg's hand on my hair stilled, then dropped down to clamp on my shoulder. It made me feel very secure. "The devil he did!"

"He's really weird. But Marita — well, I don't understand her, that's all. There's something going on, I can't figure what it is, Greg, but it makes me uneasy."

He was silent for a moment. Then he said, "You know, I've been thinking about Tiger."

My heart contracted, just hearing my dog's name.

"What you told me about his behavior doesn't make sense, does it? I mean, there must have been someone he knew up there above the trail. Have you thought about that? That would explain why he kept showing himself and barking as if he wanted you to follow him."

"I don't want to talk about it, Greg. It still hurts too much."

He straightened and let his arm fall on the seat behind my head. "I know, Janice. What I'm saying is maybe you were wrong about Mrs. Crowder?"

But I didn't want to discuss Mrs. Crowder, either. "I've got to get back. Marita was in the shower when I left. She'll be wondering why I've gone out at this time of night. Besides, it's about time for my mother to phone again."

"Okay. Just promise me once more that this is the last time you'll go down to that place with Marita."

I promised, and Greg kissed me again, a long tender kiss that made me want to cry I was so happy.

Actually, I didn't go down with Marita that weekend. Friday morning she asked me if I would drive my car down after work, as she was taking the day off to go down early and prepare for the party. I wished more than ever that Greg were able to go with me so I wouldn't have to drive alone. But I knew the way well now.

An outsize orange sun was sliding behind the coast range as I reached Casa de las Tres Hermanas, and as usual the iron gates had been left open for me. The Casa rose at the end of the tree-lined drive, red-roofed and golden-walled, topped by the bell tower, impressive in its sunbathed dignity. For a brief moment I sensed the quality of Marita's obsession. In this fiery light Casa de las Tres Hermanas was larger than life, otherworldly in its golden aura, the very substance of romance.

Then the sun, sinking lower, turned deep red. As I continued up the drive, the scene ahead of me darkened and the Casa looked for one terrible moment as if it were bathed in fresh blood.

I didn't know why I was frightened, but I had a brief urgent impulse to turn around and drive back to Santa Teresa. Then I thought of Sandy and Jerry — and Marita who must have been cooking all day ("All Sandy's favorite things, like crab cakes and chocolate mousse," she had said last night) — and knew I was being foolish.

By the time I reached the entry, the strange, bloody light had faded. It was almost dark. Several other cars were already parked around the circular drive, one of them Marita's.

"Hi!" Sandy said, giving me a quick hug when I entered.

"Sandy, I'm so happy for you. Jerry is a lucky man."

She was startled. "How did you know?"

"Marita told me."

"Marita!" Sandy looked stunned.

Oh, heavens! I'd spoiled Marita's surprise.

When I entered the kitchen, I immediately sensed tension in the air. Paul sat in the corner cradling his silent guitar. Sandy went to the hearth and, looking flushed and defiant, sat beside Jerry. Rick, greeting me, seemed edgy, with heightened color under his olive skin.

Marita, the only other person in the room, was drawn taut as a piano wire.

There's been a row, I thought, and wondered what they had quarreled about. Why did I come, when I could have stayed in Santa Teresa and written a nice note to Sandy?

"No one else is coming tonight," Marita said. "So we might as well eat."

Rick insisted on filling my plate and bringing it with his to sit so close to me on the hearth that we bumped elbows trying to eat. When I pointedly moved away, Paul hit an atonal chord, and Rick glared at him.

It was a strange evening before an engagement party, I thought, with everyone out-of-sorts.

Marita shooed us out of the kitchen after dinner, keeping Rick with her, insisting he must help her whip up her "specialty" for tomorrow. In the sitting room across the foyer from the cavernous living room, we were more relaxed. The absence of Marita and Rick brought release from the tension that had been overpowering in the kitchen. I thought, not for the first time, how alike those two were, charged with a crackling energy that attracted, yet was disquieting, too.

"Have you checked the east wing since we repaired the roof?" Paul asked Sandy.

"I think Rick has. It's like living in a museum," Sandy complained.

"There's a fortune in those neglected antiques." Paul struck a warning chord.

"We do the best we can, or —" Sandy began.

"Of course we do. It's simply too much." He emphasized that with a mournful twang of his strings, then turned to me. "You've seen the closed wings, Janice?"

"No. Rick promised me once he would show me the ballroom."

Sandy wrinkled her nose. "It's probably knee-deep in dust, with the stuffing coming out of everything and the drapes in tatters."

"I say throw it all out," Jerry muttered. "Bats and dust and rust and mildew."

"Philistines," Paul muttered. He stood, holding his guitar by its long neck. "Tell the chefs good night for me. I'll see you tomorrow."

Marita and Rick were still in the kitchen, murmuring over a steady chop-chop at the cutting board. I walked to the door with Paul, thinking to give Sandy and Jerry a few moments of privacy. When I came back they were murmuring together so seriously that I decided to go to bed. I don't think they even saw me pass the open door of the music room to climb the stair.

I lay in bed remembering Greg saying, "Then why are you going this weekend?" and wished I were with him.

But Greg was working overtime at the park.

I wished with all my heart that my mother and Kelly would come back — well, my mother, anyway. If she didn't call Sunday night when we returned to Santa Teresa, I would call her. It seemed ages since I had talked to her, and then it had been a conversation about how wonderful it was on that beach.

What were Marita and Rick discussing so seriously and so privately in the kitchen?

I reminded myself that Marita had been good to me. After all, she had enabled me to escape Mrs. Crowder that terrible day Tiger had been poisoned.

That fateful Saturday morning I slept late. So did Sandy. We met in the upstairs hall and went down together, to find Marita at the kitchen stove.

"Good morning," she said, gaily, waving a spatula at the chafing dish on the table. "Help yourselves to scrambled eggs. I've sent Rick in to Hollister for some pine nuts."

"Pine nuts?"

"For my specialty."

Sandy rolled her eyes at me. We carried our breakfast trays out on the terrace. "Let's keep out of her way," Sandy suggested, when we had finished our second cup of coffee. "Want the three-dollar tour?"

"Sure."

She took a great ring of decorative keys from one of the iron hooks on the kitchen wall, picked a flashlight out of a drawer and with a negligent wave at Marita, led the way.

"Don't get lost," Marita called after us.

Sandy laughed.

The first door she unlocked was behind the staircase at the end of the great hall that was the front entry. It opened on the courtyard I looked down into from my bedroom. It was larger than it seemed from above. Brown grass, brittle-leaved lemons in stone tubs, a dying willow tree, all looking desiccated and sick. Across the court the windows opening on it were boarded up.

"We kept this court green when Mama was alive, but . . ." Sandy shrugged.

She turned left and unlocked another door. Her sneakers made a quick shushing sound on the unglazed tile of the dark narrow gallery we entered as she hurried ahead of me, unlocking doors on each side. We stood in the doorway of one after another, giving me a few minutes for a swift look before Sandy swept me on.

There was an office in which the principal piece of furniture was a huge ornate desk with many pigeonholes. "Should be in a museum," Sandy muttered, when I admired it. "It's just rotting here."

The rooms were ill-lit behind their boarded-up windows. Some of the furniture was shrouded in muslin covers. In other rooms it was layered with dust. There was a game room, its furniture all upholstered in rotting Spanish leather.

"Rick and I spent many hours here when we were kids."

One room was so dark I could see nothing but hundreds of small winking lights when Sandy's flashlight swept it. I gasped, remembering the bats.

Sandy giggled and let the circle of her light rest in one place. Gradually I made out a saddle, heavily encrusted with engraved silver in the Spanish style. Sandy swept her flash around more slowly and I realized that all the winking lights had been reflections in brightly polished silver medallions decorating dozens of saddles and bridles.

"They must be worth a small fortune!" I exclaimed.

"Oh, they are," Sandy said, airily, "but Marita won't part with one of them. Paul and Rick spend hours in here with silver polish."

"Are the saddles ever used?"

"Not so often since we sold our horses. You should see our Rick in his charro costume. The answer to a señorita's prayer."

Yes, I thought. That skintight, black-and-silver suit with its rakish straight-brimmed black hat would suit him beautifully.

I stumbled over something, and Sandy turned her torch back at my feet. It illuminated an object which resembled an enormous fang-toothed grin, disembodied and horrible.

"Bear trap," Sandy said, and was off again with a rapid shush-shushing. I hurried to catch up with her light.

The corridor ended at a wall. There was a right turn into another long gallery, darker than the first. Sandy was far ahead of me now. As I rounded the corner, I saw the shadowy figure of a man silhouetted against Sandy's light. His arm was raised. A second later a stray reflection from Sandy's flash ricocheted from his upraised sword.

I screamed.

CHAPTER
11

SANDY laughed. She backed up and turned her flashlight full on the figure. It was an old Spanish suit of armor complete with slitted helmet, its metal tarnished black with age.

"Gruesome, isn't he? Rick rigged him up with that old sword. My brother's sense of humor."

I felt foolish. I should have realized that Sandy must have run right by the figure, because it was her light behind it that had thrown it into silhouette. "Wow, he's something!"

"Rick or the tin soldier?"

"Both."

Sandy giggled and sped off. I struggled to keep up with her, but she was moving so swiftly she left me in darkness whenever she rounded a corner.

"Slow down, can't you? I can't see where I'm going."

"Sorry. It's all old stuff to me. Rick and I used to play all over the place."

After a while I was totally confused as to where in the Casa we were. It was far larger than I had guessed. I remember going through other small courts, open to the sky. Most windows in the house, many of them boarded up, opened on inner courts. The few windows in the outer wall were heavily barred.

"It's like a prison, isn't it?"

"It's the Spanish way," Sandy said, shrugging. "The garden is always enclosed within the walls of the house."

One room was lined with massive wardrobes and old trunks. "There are still some of my great-grandmother's clothes in them," Sandy told me. "Ball gowns and tea gowns and riding habits. Rick and I loved to dress up in them when we were kids."

We went up and down stairs. From one court-yard, which had heavily bolted doors wide enough to let a carriage through, she took me into a series of small rooms with deepset shuttered windows and a bare austerity. The simple but heavy furniture was almost black. There were small niches for the Virgin Mary in the whitewashed walls, and wrought-iron candle-holders. In many rooms I saw cracked pitchers and basins and chamber pots.

"Servants' rooms," Sandy explained.

Occasionally we came out again into the light of the bright morning sky. I remember one court in which an elaborate bronze fish stood on its tail to form a fountain in a shallow pool that was bone dry. From each court we mounted a few steps.

"Where is the ballroom?" I asked, finally.

"We're coming to that." We entered the court

where the empty swimming pool opened like a single blue eye to the sky. Involuntarily I looked for the dead bird I had glimpsed among the leaves. I did not see it and I wondered what little scavenging animal had found its way into that deep corner.

Sandy unlocked a pair of heavy carved doors with wrought-iron handles and a lock of intricate design. It opened on a foyer from which a broad tiled stair rose to a second level.

Sandy ran lightly up beside the wrought-iron rail. I followed her into an immense room, ill-lit and gloomy, magnificent but sad in its faded elegance. Filmy cobwebs festooned its three huge crystal chandeliers and stretched across the long French windows, draped with faded rose velvet, that overlooked the courtyard. Pale damask chairs and sofas lined the blank wall opposite the windows.

Sandy slowed, letting me linger at last. "It's the dream of Marita's life to give a grand ball here."

She said it flatly, with no expression, but her quick humorous look made me see just how far from reality Marita's obsession had taken her. There might be a fortune in the Casa's old artifacts but Marita would need several fortunes to restore and maintain it as it once was.

Still, I could understand her passion, for I could imagine the ballroom restored to its former glamour, crystal sparkling, gold leaf gleaming, a ball with sweeping skirts in full swing. I could almost hear the music.

"The orchestra played on the dais at the end there." Sandy was pointing down the length of the room at a miniature stage, shaped like a shell, with lushly painted cupids above it. A door was set in the wall on its right.

She was moving back toward the stair. "My grandfather modernized the powder rooms at this end," she said behind me.

I had walked to one of the windows, and was looking through its film of cobwebs and dust to the court below. It was the same view I had seen from the bell tower the day Rick and I climbed to the top. Closer, the empty swimming pool looked drearier, even more neglected. Now I could see that the dead bird was still there, after all, with dusty dried leaves swirled over it.

When I turned away from the window Sandy had disappeared. "Sandy?"

She did not answer but I heard a faint sound — the soft fall of her sneakers going down the stairs.

"Sandy, wait!" I cried, remembering the dark corridors through which I had hurried after her with an irrational fear of losing my way in those interminable passages.

The light, rapid steps did not slow. I ran down the parquet floor, but when I gained the head of the stair, she was just slipping through the double doors below.

"Why are you in such a hurry?" I asked, irritated, running down the steps. Just before I reached the bottom she banged the doors shut, and I heard the heavy key turn in the lock.

"Sandy!" I wailed, in shocked disbelief. "Come back here and open this door!" I pounded as hard as I could on the heavy wood. Faintly, through it, I heard the sound of her feet running down the gallery beside the empty swimming pool.

The wood, as hard as iron, bruised my fists. "Sandy," I yelled. "This is not funny!"

She did not even pause. It had to be a joke! But Sandy — of all people!

After a while I gave up pounding and calling and climbed wearily upstairs. There was no glamour in the decaying ballroom now. Like a prison, I thought, observing again that there were no windows on the outer wall. Feeling a strange apprehension, I went to one of the windows looking down on the courtyard and tugged and pulled until I had wrenched it open. A cloud of dust flew out from its draperies.

Shuddering, I brushed at the cobwebs clinging to my arms. There was a small balcony railed with iron grillwork. I stepped out and looked down into the paved court.

It was a long way down. I could see the tiny bird in a corner of the pool more clearly now. It was long dead, nothing but a skeleton to which a few gray feathers clung. I could rot in this rotting room.

Stop it, Janice, I told myself. Sandy will be back when she has scared you half to death. Maybe she thinks she has a reason for doing something so dumb. I can't see any reason for it, but then I'm not a college girl.

I walked down the hall toward the stage, leaving my footprints in the layer of dust that covered the parquet floor. The small door at the right of the stage opened on what must have been the musicians' cloakroom. There was a second door at its rear. It opened on the landing of the stair to the bell tower!

I ran down to the door at the bottom of the stair, the door through which Rick and I had entered the day we climbed to the tower, with a lovely vision of myself walking around the house and surprising Sandy in the kitchen. "Had your fun?" I would ask, nonchalantly.

The door was locked.

It was dark down at the bottom of the narrow stair. I reached up to brush something from my hair — cobwebs? — and my hand encountered something soft and alive that was moving so swiftly I could have imagined the brief encounter. I screamed, remembering the bats.

Still screaming, I ran up to the landing, slipping around me with both hands. There must be millions of them, disturbed by my shrieks. But I forced myself to continue up the stair until I came out into the slanted sunlight of the bell tower. I looked up through the struts and braces to the iron bell hanging far above. If I rang the bell, would someone come?

Rick had tied the rope up so Carlos could not reach it. It was out of my reach, too, tied in loops just under the clapper. It looked impossibly high, and I remembered Rick saying he would have to bring up an extension ladder and ask Greg to help him tie it up.

Just then I heard a car start up somewhere out of my vision. I looked across the roofs to the drive between the rows of trees and soon Marita's car appeared, going toward the gate. I leaned over the parapet and yelled at her, praying she could hear me over the sound of her motor.

She drove on.

But where was she going? I saw her get out of her car and open the gate, then return to her car. I screamed myself hoarse but she did not even look toward the house. Beyond the gate she turned right. In that direction she could be headed for Hollister. (But Rick had gone to Hollister for her!)

What was going on? I was more alarmed than angry now.

Even driving down the road Marita would hear the bell. *If only I could ring it!* I put my foot in the angle of a supporting timber and began to climb the wooden scaffolding. The third support I tested gave way beneath my foot. The scaffolding shuddered and the bell vibrated with a high tremolo sound, but did not ring. I was falling backward, down to the hard stone floor.

I was stunned for a moment by the jolt. I had landed on one hip and it hurt painfully. My hands were full of slivers from the wooden upright I had been grasping. Slowly, I pulled myself up by the parapet, and was transfixed by what I saw.

My mother's little green car, which I had left parked at the edge of the front drive, was moving around the side of the house just below the tower. I could not see who was driving it. It continued on toward the stables, then beyond them into the woods, and disappeared.

Now I knew it was no use to call for help. My skin felt cold and my head blank with shock as I realized Sandy was not playing a practical joke. I had been deliberately locked in, and my car was being hidden.

Why?

I shrank back into a shadowed corner of the bell tower where I thought I could not be observed, and watched what I could see of the Casa's surroundings. Presently I saw Rick walking back from the stables. He disappeared around the other side of the house, going toward the kitchen terrace.

So Rick had not gone to Hollister, after all. Why had Marita lied about it? Marita could have been headed there, or for Santa Teresa. If she did not return soon I would know she had gone back to Santa Teresa.

What did that mean? What about her party? Sandy had seemed surprised that I knew. Had it all been a hoax to get me here? But for what reason?

I was nearly crazy with the questions I could not answer. And nothing else happened. I stayed in the tower in the sunshine, watching and picking slivers out of my bleeding hands, until late afternoon when the sun lay just above the coast range and dusk was deepening the shadows around the Casa. Before dark descended, I went back down the narrow stair to the landing and through the door into the ballroom. There I collapsed on a faded rose sofa, sending up little puffs of dust that made me sneeze.

I tried to tell myself that Sandy would be back when she had had her fun, but I failed to see where the fun could be, and I was very frightened. Something very strange was happening to me. While my mother, I thought bitterly, was playing love games with Kelly on that Mexican beach! If anything happened to me while she was away I would never, never forgive Kelly.

It was dark when I heard the key turn in the lock and then footsteps on the tile steps. A light was ascending the stair. Rick appeared, carrying a lantern and a bottle of wine. Sandy followed him with a tray holding food and two wine glasses.

I was on my feet, one sore hand on my bruised hip. "All right, Sandy!" I said, crossly. "What's this all about, anyway?" But the effect was spoiled when my voice trembled.

She came quickly forward and set the tray down on the sofa beside me. "Fifteen minutes!" she said sternly to Rick, and turned and ran. Not once had her eyes met mine.

I started after her, but Rick caught my arms. His grasp was so tight it numbed my hands. Once again I heard the doors creak shut and the rasp of the key.

Rick let me go, then, and we faced each other in the weird light of his lantern. His proud face, emerging from the shadows, was more than ever like a portrait of a proud young Spanish nobleman.

But his voice was quite normal. "I thought you might be hungry."

I should have been ravenous but I was too worried to feel hungry. "I don't fancy eating dust," I said. "You and Sandy have had your fun. Now let's go."

He uncorked the wine bottle — it had been opened — and filled the two glasses. ". . . and I thought we should celebrate," he continued, ignoring my outburst.

I refused the wine glass Rick held out, but picked up a sandwich. "What's to celebrate?" I was so furious with Sandy I wouldn't drink a Coke to her engagement.

"Our elopement," Rick said.

My head jerked up.

He held up his glass, blood-red in the glow from the lantern. "To the future Señora Sabin y Carrasco, the new mistress of Casa de las Tres Hermanas. Isn't that something to celebrate?"

"Is that why Sandy is giving you fifteen minutes? So you can persuade me to elope? Well, you'd need more time than that, Rick

Carrasco . . . or Sabin . . . or whatever! I'll never elope with you!"

"You have no choice," he said, with that arrogance that was so annoying. "You must marry me because your money is necessary for the restoration of the Casa. Don't you see?"

I stared. "Are you crazy, Rick? I have no money."

There was a frightening change in his eyes. "Didn't I tell you never to call me crazy!"

Heavens, what a temper. I made a mental note. Rick was crazy but I'd better not tell him.

"We know about the money," he said. "The old man is dying and Weldon has seen his will. Weldon's law firm drew it up."

I was still gaping. "What old man? What are you talking about?"

"Your father's half-brother. My uncle. He's very rich and he never married. My father was his only close relative, but he's cut us out of his will because he disapproved of my father.

"We won't stand for it, Janice. You have no right to the money — it didn't come from grandfather. Uncle Barry made every penny of it himself, and you are no relation to him. So it is rightfully ours, you see? Weldon says the simplest way out is for you to marry me."

Weldon! Was he back of all this craziness? "Hah! When hell freezes."

"If you refuse, we'll get the money some other way. But we'll get it. We have to have it for the Casa. You understand, don't you, Janice?"

I didn't understand. I didn't believe him. I

had never heard my father speak of any half-brothers. I wondered if Rick had been drinking.

He had ruined my appetite. I had taken a few bites of my sandwich but now I put it down. Again he offered me my wine glass; again I refused it.

"Fine. We'll make better use of our time." He set both glasses down on the floor then tried to take me in his arms. I dropped my sandwich and jumped to my feet.

He grabbed me again and held me while I kept turning my head, avoiding the kisses that fell on my cheek, my ear, my hair. When he dropped his head and lightly bit my neck, I wrenched myself out of his embrace and gave him a hard smack that I aimed at his temple but that, because he turned his head, bloodied his nose.

His head flew back, eyes blazing, and he struck me a stinging blow on the side of my face with the flat of his hand. It rocked my head. I screamed.

Sandy came running up the stair, crying, "Rick, you promised." Her face registered shock when she saw her brother. Blood was streaming from Rick's nose.

He groped for a handkerchief. "Don't ever strike me again!" he warned me, his eyes as hard as stones, then went swiftly toward Sandy.

I ran after them, my head ringing, my eyes blurred with tears of pain. Before I could catch them Sandy was pushing Rick ahead of her through the doors. She cast one anxious glance up at me then slipped through herself. The key turned. I was locked in again.

I stopped where I was, halfway down the stairs. I couldn't believe what was happening. Rick had thoroughly frightened me. I was bewildered, not understanding anything, but the fact that my car had been hidden seemed ominous.

How long did they plan to keep me here? Until I agreed to an elopement? Was Marita in the plot, too? She must be, if Weldon was. She had gone back to Santa Teresa, leaving me with her beloved crazy nephew. And Sandy — and I had thought Sandy was my friend!

Greg had been right about them. None of them was my friend. And Greg, who *was* my friend, was miles away in Santa Teresa. If I were to escape the Casa I would have to do it myself.

Slowly I climbed back up the stairs. That fantastic story about my father's half-brother was incomprehensible. Truthfully, I did not know much about my father's boyhood. He had never said much about his family, and I had not been that interested.

I was beginning to feel claustrophobic in the shabby, filthy ballroom. Forcing myself to brave the bats and the darkness, I opened the door to the bell tower landing. There was a moon, for its bluish light glimmered on the top steps. Slowly and cautiously, my hip hurting me, I climbed toward the moonlight.

I could sense the movement of the bats, who

can navigate perfectly at night. They were darting about, fanning the air but moving so fast I could not see them except when they crossed a beam of light, and then it was just a whisk of a shadow.

When I reached the top the moon shone in through the arches under the bell. A few lights visible above the dark eucalyptus trees marked the subdivision below the rancho, and there was a glow emanating from the front wing of the house where lights were on. I could see the moon now, a pale three-quarters of a platter rising above the trees. All else around me was in darkness.

I crossed to the other side of the tower and presently distinguished a faint glow to the rear of the Casa which must come from the stables. They were closer to the tower than the front wing where Rick and Sandy lived. I remembered then that Carlos might have extra keys to the door at the base of the tower.

How could I reach him? Would he come if he heard me call? With his scrambled brains and his imperfect English, could he understand what I wanted of him?

Then I had an inspiration. I began singing "The Song of Three Sisters," the faintly sad, faintly minor Spanish song Paul had taught us. I sang it over and over. Carlos might not understand my words, but he must recognize the tune. Surely he would wonder why someone was singing in the bell tower and come to investigate?

It seemed hours; perhaps it was fifteen or

twenty minutes before I saw him cautiously emerge from his stable quarters. I lost him in the shadows and I did not hear his approach. I just looked down and saw the trembling old man staring up at the bell tower.

"Open the door for me, Carlos," I called, softly.

He shuddered and crossed himself. "Is that you, Consuela?" he quavered.

Consuela? Was she one of the tragic Three Sisters?

"Yes," I said, crossing my fingers.

But it was the wrong answer. Carlos pointed a trembling finger at me and said, "Go back to your bed, wicked girl. Do not ask my help in your disobedience."

"Carlos, I am imprisoned here. Find your key and open the door at the bottom of the tower."

"Devil woman!" he cried, in sudden rage. "Go back where you came from and leave me in peace!"

"Carlos, I have done nothing wicked. They are wicked. They have locked me in. Carlos, please . . ."

"No more. Ask no more of me, I pray." His brief rage had dissolved in tears. He covered his eyes and mumbled, "I am an old man. Leave me in peace, Consuela."

"Carlos, don't go," I pleaded. "Listen to me. Get your key."

"Leave me in peace, Consuela. Leave me, leave me."

The old man was gone. I was crying now. I

stumbled down the steps, slapping futilely at the bats skimming my hair, and returned to the ballroom. I felt dizzy and sick.

By the time I reached the nearest sofa my legs were as limp as wet noodles. I was so woozy I realized I was not thinking straight, and I wondered what was wrong with me. Was it hunger? I had eaten nothing since breakfast but the one or two bites I had taken from the sandwich Sandy had brought me.

Rick had left the wine glasses on the floor, both still full. Funny. I thought he had been drinking wine. I picked up the glass he had poured for me. Perhaps it would clear my head. I swallowed a mouthful of it. Then a warning light flashed somewhere behind my eyes, and I thought, *Suppose I am being drugged?*

My heart was pounding so hard I could feel it pushing my blood up the side of my throat and into my head, and I wondered if it was the wine causing it or sheer terror. In the desperate clarity of sudden panic I understood what Rick could have been saying when he told me that they would get the money, one way or another.

Suppose I *was* named in his uncle's will? I could not believe him, but just suppose it were true. If I died, couldn't Sandy and Rick claim the money, as his next-of-kin?

I had no way of knowing if it were legally possible, but once the thought occurred to me, I was panic-stricken. I staggered up from the sofa and made my uncertain way toward the French window I had forced open, determined to risk breaking a leg jumping down to the paved court below, even though I feared there was no way for me to get out of the courtyard.

I vaguely remember an insane plan to hide myself under the heaped leaves in the swimming pool, like the skeleton bird that haunted me. The last conscious memory I have is of slumping to the parquet floor and inhaling dust.

CHAPTER
12

IT was very quiet. The air smelled fresh and sweet and somehow familiar, with no trace of eucalyptus oil in it. Mountain air, I thought, drowsily. I heard a sleepy bird twitter.

Voices wakened me as I was sinking back into sleep. They came from far above me. ". . . as long as her mother knows," Mrs. Crowder said.

Mrs. Crowder?

I opened my eyes. My vision was blurred but I thought I was in my car, but not behind the wheel. I was in the passenger seat. A faint red glow colored the darkness. It took me a few seconds to identify it. What was I doing parked down below Mr. Crowder's BAR AND EATS? I felt strangely heavy-headed.

I wakened again when Rick opened the door and slid behind the wheel.

Rick? What a crazy dream I was having! I closed my eyes again and heard the whir of the starter and then the purr and vibration of the motor as he drove away.

I was vaguely aware that he had turned

around and we were descending, going around curves. The swaying and the fresh cool air began to revive me. I was not dreaming. I was in my mother's car with Rick at the wheel. My memory was returning, piece by piece. I'd been at Casa de las Tres Hermanas, hadn't I? Yes! Locked in the ballroom!

There'd been talk of an elopement, I remembered, with alarm . . . Sandy had brought me food . . . Sandy, my false friend!

Had Rick abducted me?

I considered that, feeling woozy and somewhat nauseous as the car lurched, going too fast around the curves. The wine Rick brought me must have been drugged — probably the sandwich, too. Thank heaven I had only tasted them!

I was alarmed enough now to see that I had better not let Rick know I was awake until I figured out what he was up to.

Why had he driven to my apartment and talked with Mrs. Crowder? Or had I dreamed that? If I hadn't been dreaming, what had he told her?

". . . as long as her mother knows," I'd heard Mrs. Crowder say. Knows what?

Of course! He must have told Mrs. Crowder that we had my mother's permission to elope. But Mrs. Crowder had sounded uncomfortable. She would likely call my mother about this. Surely Rick must have realized she would do that. It dawned on me that he must have had a good reason for stopping at the apartment.

My fuzzy mind worried over the question while we descended into the still warm air of the valley. We were returning toward Santa Teresa, weren't we?

Why?

And why had Rick wanted to stop at the apartment? What had he done there? Of course! Packed some clothes for me! A girl can't elope without clothes, can she?

But I had clothes at Marita's in Santa Teresa. She wanted me to marry Rick, yet he had not gone there. So Rick had another reason for going to Mt. Eustis Lodge. Was it because he knew Mrs. Crowder would call my mother?

That started my heart to pound so loudly that I was afraid Rick would hear it. Oh, Greg, Greg, if only I had listened to you about this one last weekend. It may be my *last*.

As soon as the thought flashed through my mind, I felt a deadly chill. That was it. Rick wanted the Crowders to know we were eloping. He *wanted* them to call my mother. He wanted everyone to know. Because then when something happened to me, everyone would believe it was an accident. And there would be no obstacle between Rick and his uncle's money.

I tried not to believe I was in deadly danger of losing my life, but I was terrified. I made an effort to keep my breathing even and my head cool in spite of the terror that nearly paralyzed me. I must not let Rick know that I was conscious.

It was not easy to pretend to be sleeping in

a car going around curves on a mountain road. Rick had secured my seatbelt, but it was still difficult not to brace myself against the curves, to stay relaxed enough to roll with them; especially difficult because my mind was fluttering like a caged bird's wings, trying to find some way of escape. I had to discover where Rick was taking me.

Had he said something to Mrs. Crowder about driving all night? I had been so drowsy when I first wakened that I was not sure what I had heard.

Rick solved my problem for me. He braked to a stop and my heart jumped into my throat. Here it comes, I thought. But he made a U-turn, doused his lights — I could tell through my closed eyelids when the dash lights went off — and started back up the mountain. I was baffled. Where in the world was he taking me?

The lights came back on after we passed the lodge. I concentrated on the road, following every turn in my mind. It was only a ten-minute drive from the lodge to the park entrance, and I had hiked over most of the way.

The county park where Greg works spreads over the crest of the mountain, which is a part of the coast range, and only about fifteen hundred feet in elevation. The park, I happened to know, is a day facility, locked up tight at night to keep the beer-drinking vandals out. None of the rangers would be on duty. I had no idea what time it was, but I knew Rick would have to cut a wire fence to get a car in or out of the park after nine o'clock.

Rick slowed and I opened my eyes just in time to see the entrance kiosk flash past. He did not stop.

From there the road turns left and descends sharply to make a loop down through a small valley and climb another gradual slope to the west entrance of the park. When Rick continued past that entrance, too, I knew where he was heading. From the west entrance there is a steep section of narrow road that snakes down a drop-off of twelve or thirteen hundred feet. It then levels out into a road that gradually climbs to a little-traveled ridge route through the Santa Cruz Mountains to the coast. I had driven over it one Sunday with Kelly and my mother when the wild flowers were in bloom.

Now I thought I knew what was in Rick's mind, and I shivered. It made such a credible story — if he could make everyone believe I was willing to marry him.

He must have told Mrs. Crowder we were going to drive to someplace in Nevada — Las Vegas or Lake Tahoe — where we could be married without waiting for a license. That's where my mother would send someone, the police, maybe, to stop us. Later Rick would admit, with that beautiful arrogance that has its own charm, that he hadn't wanted to confess we were first going to spend the night in Santa Cruz.

Only we would never reach Santa Cruz. Something terrible would happen, something Rick would survive.

I was not sure it was the right scenario, but it was all I had to act on, and I had better think fast. *What I was going to do?*

The air had changed. It was no longer fresh and cool, with the tang of pine. It had a sharp, smoky smell, like a campfire but so much stronger that it was beginning to smart in my nostrils. I lifted my lashes a fraction and ventured a glance out of my window. What lay beyond it was totally obscured by smoke! Even while I looked we drove through the billowing cloud and out into the clear, star-hung night, but before I closed my eyes again the mountainside was obscured by another patch of smoke.

A forest fire?

Marita had said the forest service was fighting several blazes in the Santa Cruz Mountains. One must be burning close to the boundaries of Mt. Eustis Park. We were swinging around hairpin curves now, and I visualized the long drop down into the canyon. The smoke was heavier as we descended. Surely Rick could not be driving into a fire! The thought of being trapped in a burning forest came, so terrifying that my blood froze.

Fighting my panic, I asked myself what Greg's logical mind would make of this. Immediately I became calmer. Rick would not drive into something he could not get out of. If the danger from the forest fire were extreme the road would be blocked to traffic. So the fire was not immediately threatening, except in the way Rick might use it to his advantage. Perhaps I could find an advantage in it, too.

I had no time to speculate on that because Rick pulled abruptly over to the wrong side of the road, and I knew the time had come. Carefully, I released my seatbelt.

Rick braked the car but he did not take it out of gear. When he opened his door and jumped out on the shoulder, his foot left the brake and the car continued to roll. The lights were still on, and one swift glance told me I was headed for the smoke-filled canyon. My scenario was right, then.

Almost as soon as Rick jumped, I had unlatched my door. When my feet touched the pavement I was running, running for my life. I had gained not only the advantage of complete surprise, but I had jumped directly on the roadway while Rick was still trying to get out of the way of the moving car without going over the edge.

I could hear my mother's little car crashing down the rocky slope to its destruction. Now the fire was my guardian, for in half a dozen running steps I reached a wall of smoke dense enough to swallow me.

I tried to close my ears to the horrible noises of smashing metal and snapping trees echoing in the canyon. Over them I heard Rick swearing in Spanish. I could not see him but I could hear him running after me, and I knew with his long legs he could outrun me.

If I could hear him, he could hear me. He was following my footsteps. I reached down and pulled off a shoe, and heard Rick swear when he stumbled over it.

I pulled off my other shoe and tucked it in the pocket of my jacket. It might do as a weapon. Now my feet made no sound. The silence in the canyon, now that the car had stopped rolling, was worse than the noises of crunching metal and crashing trees. There was only the low gurgle of the creek far below us and the steady pound of Rick's feet coming after me.

"Janice!" he called. He was so close I could hear his heavy breathing. "I tossed your shoe into the canyon, Janice."

Then he stopped . . . to listen?

"Janice?" Perhaps he could not tell whether I had left the road or not, and was trying to trick me into answering.

I was breathing hard and there was a sharp pain in my side, but I kept running. He must have picked up some sound, for he came on.

The smoke was like thick fog. I could see nothing but I ran on, down the hairpin curves of the narrow road. Why didn't a car come along the way I was running? Someone — anyone — who could take me far away from Rick's relentless pursuit, away from the steady, pounding, long strides I could never hope to evade.

I was becoming exhausted, and the smoke was painful to my lungs. But now the pall of smoke was thinning. I could see more of the road that separated the steep mountainside from the steeper drop into the canyon.

Rick was still hidden behind me but I could hear his footfalls as he came swiftly on. In a moment he would burst out of the smoke and I would be as visible as the bright moon which had risen and was shining through the trees above us.

And there was no place to hide.

CHAPTER
13

T HERE was no smoke now.
I could see the shoulders of the road. It
was flattening out into a longer straight stretch,
and the darkness at its end was beginning to
look like a hillside. For a moment I panicked,
thinking I was running toward a dead end.

But the feel of the road under my stocking
feet had changed, and there was a cool, moist
breeze rising. I realized I had entered the narrow
concrete bridge which took the road across the
gorge where it made a sharp turn to continue
down the other side of the stream. From far
below the bridge I could hear the water, rippling
over large stones.

Suddenly I felt very exposed, realizing my
danger if Rick should overtake me on the bridge.
There was no place to go but down, no room to
dodge the attack I feared would come. I ran on,
as silently as I could, but I knew that I could
not run much longer, and my gasping breaths
must be revealing where I was. If only I could

gain the end of the bridge while Rick was still invisible in the smoke! Perhaps on the other side I could find a place to hide.

It was a forlorn hope, but my only one.

At last I was across the bridge and at the point where the road turned sharply right to follow the gorge. Ahead of me on my left was a mountainside too steep to climb; on my right the road dropped off a hundred and fifty feet to the rock-strewn stream below. Although the road sloped in the direction I was going, I was too winded to go on. There was nothing to do but go under the bridge and hope Rick would think I was still silently running.

A glance over my shoulder told me he was still enveloped in the pall of smoke I had come through. I crept off the roadway, clinging to the bridge as I felt for footing on the sloping ledge of rock to which the concrete arch was anchored.

When my foot dislodged a large rock and I lost my balance, panic destroyed my last shred of caution. I screamed.

Shaking, I clung to the bridge while the stone rolled down the hillside and my scream came echoing back in waves from the canyon. Now Rick knew exactly where I was.

A muffled splash, louder than the gurgle of the stream, told me when the stone hit bottom. My first shock of despair passed as it occurred to me that Rick might think *I* had fallen. Carefully, I inched my body into the crevice beneath the roadway, between concrete and rock. Now

I must lie without stirring, almost without breathing. It was my only chance.

Rick had entered the bridge — I could tell from the hollow echo of his steps in the canyon. He came across slowly, pausing at intervals, perhaps to try to see over the side to the creek below, perhaps to listen for some sound that might reveal where I was.

I wished my heart were not beating so loudly.

Finally he went on, passing my hiding place, following the descending road. He was heading farther and farther away from any place where he might find a telephone. I remembered this well, because when Kelly had driven us over this road in his Thunderbird we had nearly starved looking for a place to eat.

But Rick might not be looking for a telephone. I reminded myself that he did not dare report an accident as long as he thought I was alive and could deny his story. Once he convinced himself I had fallen from the bridge, he would return this way and if no car came before morning would likely climb back up to the park entrance where he could tell his lies to the rangers in the morning, when they reported to work.

Greg, too — dear God, would I ever see Greg again? Or my mother?

Rick must be wondering how he would explain why my body lay in the creek some distance from where the car had gone over. Would he crawl down to the stream to try to find me and make certain I could not contradict him?

I trembled. But I had no choice but to remain where I was, cramped and shivering, scarcely daring to breathe.

I could no longer hear Rick, yet I had a suffocating sense of his nearness. I strained, listening for any telltale sound. After what seemed an interminable time, the sound I heard was that of a car approaching!

It was coming down to the bridge the way we had come. I did not dare let one car go by, for few motorists came this way at night. I had to move with care lest I slip on the loose rocks under the bridge, but I did not care now about the pebbles that rolled down into the stream. They would reveal my hiding place if Rick heard them, but it would not matter if only I could flag that passing motorist!

I reached the roadway too late. The car was already across the bridge when I emerged, and going down the opposite grade in the direction Rick was walking. It was a dark sedan, and it looked like dozens of other older cars on the road. There were three persons in the front seat, I thought, but the car was going around the first curve before I could be sure.

Would they stop to give Rick a ride? Or would he let it go by so he could determine for himself whether I was still alive? My heart sank at the thought of crawling under the bridge again. I decided to cross to the other side of the canyon and lose myself in the smoke before Rick turned back.

I wished now I had not thrown away my

shoe. My stockings were already in tatters, and
tiny pebbles, invisible in the darkness, were
bruising my feet with every step.

I ran, not daring to stop to listen for the car
which had apparently gone beyond my hearing.
Or had it stopped? I was in the center of the
bridge when I heard a car approaching behind
me.

I had no place to go. The lights impaled me.
The car stopped. It was the same dark sedan.
Jerry was driving, with Sandy and Greg beside
him.

Greg?

In the back seat was Rick!

I was transfixed with horror, hardly aware
that they were gaping at me as if I were a ghost.

Then Greg exclaimed, "Janice!" and jumped
out of the car, holding out his arms.

I backed away from him, shaking with terror.

"Don't move!" he said sharply.

I had been backing toward the gorge. I
stopped, swaying, and Greg grabbed me. "Janice,
are you all right?" His voice was gravelly, but
his arms were comforting. I leaned against him,
trembling.

"Oh, thank God, Janice! Rick thought you
went over the side with the car. He said you were
driving."

I shook my head, and pointed a shaky finger
at Rick. "He tried to kill me."

"He *what*?"

Rick was leaning out of the back window.

"She must be out of her head, Baxter! Look, she's had a bad fall —"

"Sandy, too," I stammered. "She locked me in the ballroom."

"Honey, it was Sandy who called Jerry," Greg said. He was still holding me, looking puzzled.

What did he mean Sandy had called Jerry? Called to tell him what? Not what she had done!

I held out my scratched hands with the dried blood on my palms. "I tried to reach the bell rope and the support gave way."

Greg's face reflected horror, but Rick said, "See? She's scratched her hands climbing out of the gorge. She must have been thrown out —"

"They d—drugged me," I insisted. "When I woke up I was in the car with Rick. I pretended I was still asleep, and when he pointed the car at the drop-off and got out . . ."

"Are you saying that he deliberately crashed your car?" There was disbelief in Greg's face. "Why would he do that?"

"Why?" Rick echoed, violently. "We were *eloping*, Baxter!"

"He left the car in gear and got out," I said steadily, "so I jumped out on the road and ran. He —" My voice choked up, and Greg's arms tightened around me. "He chased me and I hid under the bridge."

Greg put a hand behind my head and pushed my face into his shoulder. I was afraid he did not believe me, that he was only pitying me. But when he spoke his voice above my head was hard and cold as ice. "What have you got to say, Carrasco?"

"She's delirious. She was driving. It was her car, after all. She must have fallen out when it first turned over. I thought she was in the gulch."

"He's lying, Greg!" I was beating my fists against his chest. "Sandy, *you* know he's lying!"

Jerry, still behind the wheel, was looking grim. Sandy looked sick.

Greg let go of me. He opened the door of the car and reached in for Rick. "Come out where I can see your face when I talk to you, Carrasco, and you'd better tell the truth. Did you deliberately crash that car? With Janice in it?"

Rick crawled out of the back seat. He looked pale. "Lay off, will you, Baxter? I've just been in an accident. I think the steering failed. I can show you where the car went over. It's just up the hill a little way. When I saw what was happening, I jumped. It's a miracle that Janice is alive."

"I think you're lying," Greg told him. "Whoever was driving that car got out before it went over the edge. He sure as hell couldn't get out afterward!"

"Obviously, you don't know what you're talking about," Rick said, in his most arrogant voice.

That was when Greg hit him. In another minute they were fighting all over the road in the headlights of the car. Jerry hopped out, leaving his car sitting in the center of the road, lights blazing, but he just stood beside the car, watching Greg and Rick.

Sandy stayed in the front seat, looking wan and ill. Just the way I felt. I sank down against the bridge railing and huddled there as Greg and Rick slugged each other. Rick was taller than Greg, but Greg was broader in the shoulders and in good condition because of his summer job. Just the same, I had a sick feeling watching them stagger from rail to rail of the narrow bridge one hundred and fifty feet above the stream.

"Stop them, Jerry," I begged. "Can't you see Rick is desperate? Rick will fight dirty because he knows he has to win."

"Greg doesn't need help — yet. I don't want to get in his way."

I was still trembling and I laid my head on my knees, cradling it with my arms, unable to watch.

Gradually, I was aware of more light sweeping down behind them. Another car, coming down the grade. I raised my head. There was not room to pass and it drew up and stopped, facing Jerry's car. Then I saw it was a sheriff's car. Now Greg and Rick were fighting in a small arena lit by the four headlights. They were fighting more slowly, breathing heavily.

Jerry walked toward the car as the sheriff got out, a tall man with a face shadowed by a wide-brimmed hat, wearing a heavy gunbelt around his waist. The man riding with him who got out on the other side was Tony Kapel!

"All right, boys, break it up," the sheriff called.

Over Greg's shoulder Rick saw the sheriff's hand on his gun and froze.

Greg's blow was already on its way. It connected with Rick's chin. Rick fell backward to the pavement, and lay still.

CHAPTER
14

THE sheriff put away his gun as he and Tony bent over Rick. "An accident — it was an accident," Rick mumbled, and then we were all talking at once, shouting him down.

The sheriff was a patient man. He listened to our stories and took our names and addresses and our ages. Rick was sitting on the pavement where he had fallen when Greg hit him. He looked dazed and made no resistance when the sheriff pulled him to his feet, and had him lean on Jerry's car while he searched him for weapons and put handcuffs on him.

"Where did the car go over?"

"About a quarter of a mile up the road," Rick said.

The sheriff put Rick in his car, then walked up the road with a powerful flashlight. When he found the place, he stopped and threw a beam of light down the path that the car had made down the hillside.

When he came back, he said, "I want statements from all of you. Who is driving?"

"It's my car," Jerry said.

"Follow me to my office. This young lady will have to press charges."

"Do I have to?" I croaked.

"Yes," Tony said, firmly.

"I'll have my office call your parents so they can meet you there."

He had his radio mike in his hand before I could say, "My mother's in Mexico on her honeymoon."

"She's flying up on the next plane," Tony told the sheriff. He turned to me. "I've talked to her, Janice. She'll be here sometime tomorrow. Kelly is staying to drive his car back."

His solidity and air of authority were comforting. Again I wondered how my mother could have worked for Tony Kapel and not fallen in love with him.

"What did you tell my mother?"

"That you were eloping with Rick. That's what we thought, then. We'll call her from the sheriff's office and you can tell her yourself it wasn't true."

"But how did you know?"

He smiled at me and laid a hand on my shoulder. "Ask your boyfriend." He smiled at Greg and patted my shoulder, then strode through the beams from Jerry's headlights to the sheriff's car.

I gave a long, shuddering sigh as the sheriff backed his car off the bridge and to a wider spot where he could turn around. When they drove off, climbing the winding road to the park entrance, Rick was in the backseat, alone, behind a wire screen.

Greg and I crawled into the backseat of the sedan. He opened his arms and I settled myself against his shoulder. From that haven I told Sandy, "All right, now, talk!"

She turned to look over the front seat at me and I saw the tears on her cheeks. "Janice, you must believe I meant you no harm." She wiped her eyes with a tissue. "The whole idea was to persuade you to elope with Rick. Abducting you was Rick's brainstorm. I knew nothing about it, I swear it, Janice, and I am sure Marita didn't either."

"Marita asked me down to celebrate your engagement."

"Is that what she told you?" Sandy gasped. She and Jerry exchanged looks.

". . . and then she drove off, leaving me to Rick's mercy!"

"Marita," Sandy said, bitterly, "couldn't imagine an abduction would be necessary. She thinks nobody, but nobody, can resist her Rick."

"*You* locked me in the ballroom," I accused her. "And you brought me drugged food."

"I didn't know it was drugged. Rick asked me to play a little trick on you. He said that if he had fifteen minutes alone with you he could persuade you to elope. I agreed rather than fight with him. He can be so —" She broke off what she had been going to say, and an appalled look swiftly crossed her face and was gone, as if she

153

only then fully realized what Rick had tried to do.

"I was furious with him when he struck you," she went on, in a subdued voice. "When I locked you in the second time I was hoping to keep Rick out."

"He hit you?" Greg said, angrily. "I wish I'd smashed his pretty nose!"

"You did all right." Jerry chuckled.

"That's hard to believe," I told Sandy.

"It's true, Janice," Jerry said. "If Sandy had not walked around the house when she did and happened to see Rick carrying you to the car, Rick would have got away with . . . with whatever he was planning."

"He was planning to murder me!"

Greg's arms tightened around me. I could hear his heart, beating fast and hard.

"He must have had a duplicate key to the tower. He must have been planning this for days." Sandy's voice cracked, and Jerry took his hand off the wheel and touched her cheek. Ahead of us the red lights of the sheriff's car disappeared, then appeared again as we rounded a curve.

"She called me and told me she was worried," Jerry continued for Sandy. "So we tried to figure out, between the two of us, where Rick might be taking you. But we figured he was hustling you into an elopement."

"I said you would want to stop to get some clothes." Sandy had control of her voice again.

"And since Marita was all for an elopement and you had some clothes there, we thought —"

"So I called Greg," Jerry put in.

"And I hotfooted it over to Marita's," Greg said against my ear. "And *she* couldn't hide how pleased she was at my news. She didn't seem exactly surprised, either. That made me mad. So I called Tony, and you know what?"

"What?"

"He'd just finished talking to your mother. Mrs. Crowder had called her! Your mother called Tony to ask him to find you and Rick and bring you back. She said to call in the sheriff for help if he needed it."

"I knew Mrs. Crowder would call my mother!" I made a mental apology to her. She might be a bore, but she was not really stupid. And wasn't I fortunate to have so many friends concerned about me, willing to do something to save me from what they thought could be disaster but had no idea could cost me my life? I felt very humble, and was filled with love for all of them.

"But how did you know where Rick had taken me?"

"Oh, Mr. Crowder helped out there. He saw Rick come back without any lights. He must keep a pretty sharp eye peeled up there in his BAR AND EATS," Jerry said, with a chuckle. "And you know something? He was suspicious of Rick, because he left you sitting in the car and went in and packed your clothes himself. Said he'd never known a woman who would let someone else pick out her trousseau. I thought he was an old crock; I just couldn't believe . . ."

I had misjudged Mr. Crowder, too. I hated to admit Kelly Porter had been right when he had advised me to reserve judgement. If the Crowders had not talked to my mother and the sheriff, how would anyone have known where to find me? I shivered, reliving those tense minutes under the bridge when I had heard Rick crossing slowly above me, stopping to listen for any sound that would give me away, intent on my death. Greg felt my shiver, and his lips moved against my hair.

Now I was inclined to believe Mr. Crowder was right when he insisted his wife was not a dog poisoner. But if she did not poison Tiger, who did?

Could it have been Rick?

There was the night someone had paused outside my bedroom door at Casa de la Tres Hermanas, rousing Tiger. Had that frenzied barking sealed Tiger's death warrant? Was he killed because he was my protector?

And the prowler at the lodge when Mrs. Crowder had wondered if I were entertaining Greg? Surely that could not have been Rick! I had barely met him when that happened.

We were passing the lodge now, all in darkness except for the red neon sign. I resolved to return and apologize to both of the Crowders as soon as I could.

A half-hour later we pulled up in front of

Santa Teresa's county building. The sheriff got out of his car just ahead of us and opened the door for Rick. Taking him by the arm, the sheriff motioned us to follow. Tony fell back to enter the building with us.

"Wait here," said the sheriff, and took Rick through a door.

It was a rather drab waiting room, with a few torn magazines scattered about on the empty plastic chairs. There was a telephone booth in one corner, and Sandy made for it. When she came back, Tony said, "Let's call your mother, Janice."

The relaxation from those tense hours with Rick had left me trembling with fatigue. "You tell her about the car, Tony," I begged.

"Not up to it?"

I shook my head.

"Okay." He took a slip of paper from his wallet and made a credit call to Mexico. My mouth went dry when I heard him ask for Mrs. Kelly Porter. How could I live with that? Well, I thought, *I* still had my father's name, and I would not change it. That was one thing I could do for him.

A moment later Tony was talking to my mother. I stood just outside the door of the booth, leaning against Greg while I listened to Tony.

"Janice is here beside me, waiting to speak with you. . . . No, there was no marriage, but there was an accident . . . No one was hurt. But your car is in a ravine up by Mt. Eustis Park . . .

I haven't seen it but I would guess it's totaled . . . We're at the sheriff's office. Rick has been arrested, and the sheriff is taking statements . . . I think perhaps that had better wait for your arrival. I'll meet your plane."

He unclipped his pen from his shirt pocket and scribbled on the piece of paper that carried my mother's hotel and phone number. "Got it," he said. "Now, here's Janice."

"Hello?" I said, weakly.

"Are you all right, Janice?" Warm relief flowed through me, just hearing her familiar voice.

"I'm fine, Mother."

"You sound funny. You're not worried about the car, are you, dear? You're safe, that's what matters to me."

"I'm supposed to file charges against Rick," I told her, shakily.

"What kind of charges?"

Tony was frowning at me but I knew I had to answer her now. "Kidnapping, I think. And . . . and attempted murder."

"Oh, my God! Put Tony back on."

"Mother, I'm fine, honest."

"I'm very glad, dear, but I want to talk to Tony."

I handed him the telephone. "I thought it best to let you have a night's sleep before you heard her story," he told her. "I don't know myself exactly what happened. But Janice is okay, honestly. She's exhausted, and she still has to make her statement, but she came through unscathed. That's what I wanted you to know tonight."

He handed me the phone again. "It's a long story," I began.

My mother interrupted me. "Where's Marita?"

"I don't know. She left the Casa before . . . before I did."

"Are you staying with her tonight?"

"I don't know. I guess not. But my things are there."

"Let me talk to Tony again. My plane gets in around noon. I'll see you then, and you can tell me everything. You're really all right?"

"I'm fine, really."

A tremor came into her voice. "I love you, darling."

"Oh, Mother, don't get mushy. I'm *all right!*"

I heard Kelly saying something in the background, and my mother laughed. "Kelly says to tell you he forgives you for interrupting his honeymoon. He thinks now he'll get another."

"Oh–h–h–h," I said, furious, and handed the telephone back to Tony. Darn Kelly, anyway!

Greg turned me toward the deputy sheriff, who was beckoning me.

CHAPTER
15

I had just turned to follow the deputy when the outside door opened and Marita swept in. She was holding a light coat tightly around her as if to conceal that she had dressed hastily. She looked distraught, almost haggard, her hair windblown. Sandy had called her, of course.

Her eyes swept over Sandy and Jerry, raked Greg and Tony, and then came to rest on me.

From across the room, the deputy sheriff reminded me, "The sheriff is waiting to take your statement, Miss Litton."

Marita's eyes suddenly glistened with an anguish so intense that I shivered. Without a word to any of us, she swung around to the information officer's desk.

"I can't stay with her tonight," I whispered.

"No," Greg said.

"This way, Miss Litton." The deputy opened a door and ushered me into an office. Another man sat beside his desk. The deputy took the chair behind it and indicated one for me.

"I understand you were in an accident to-night."

"Yes, sir."

"How are you feeling now?"

"Okay."

"Just tell me in your own words exactly what happened. Officer Jarman will turn on his tape recorder. When you have finished, he will bring you a typed copy of what you have told us so you can check it for errors, and sign it. Then you can go home."

I nodded, wetting my lips. It took about half an hour. Officer Jarman picked up his tape and left the room without saying anything.

The deputy sat back in his chair. "That's a very serious charge you're making, Miss Litton."

I nodded. "What will happen to Rick?"

"He will likely be released on bail. The accident will be investigated, and the persons you have mentioned will be questioned. If the evidence gathered supports your charges, Rick could be indicted for assault with intent to do bodily harm."

"What would that mean?"

"Prison, if he is convicted."

Even after what he had done, the thought of Rick in prison upset me.

When Officer Jarman came back, the sheriff followed him. He was looking at my statement, several long typewritten sheets of paper. "Do you realize the gravity of these charges, Miss Litton?"

"Yes, sir."

"I understand your mother is flying in to-morrow. I can hold this statement overnight so she can come in with you tomorrow and you can sign it then. Would you like me to do that?"

"Yes, sir."

When I went back to the waiting room, I was trembling with fatigue. Tony and Greg stood up.

"We're taking you to the hospital," Tony said. "Your mother thinks you should have a checkup."

"Now, wait a minute," I began, indignantly.

"She is worried about the drug Rick gave you. We don't know what it was or how much you had. Neither Sandy nor Jerry have any idea what Rick used, they say."

"But I'm okay," I protested, stubbornly.

"You're exhausted," Tony said, gently, "and much too pale. We think a hospital is the best place for you tonight."

There was no way out. They took me to the emergency entrance and before long I was sitting on the edge of a bed in a curtained space, wait-ing for a doctor.

The one who came in looked absurdly young, not much older than Rick. "Your stockings are a mess," he told me cheerfully, taking out his stethoscope.

A mess? They were in tatters from scrambling over rocks, but he didn't need to remind me. "Who cares?" I muttered. "I'm alive."

"Are you sure? I haven't examined you yet." He could joke with me, with people bleeding and babies crying all around us.

"If you're a real doctor instead of an intern, you should grow a beard," I told him, but he just laughed and went on poking at me as if I were a head of lettuce.

"What drug did you take?"

"I didn't take it. It was in the food and drink that was given to me. I passed out."

"For how long?"

"I've no idea."

Finally, he decided to keep me overnight for observation. I was put in a wheelchair and bundled off to a room, which I shared with an elderly black woman.

"You'll be safe here," Greg had whispered, when he kissed me good-bye. But I spent a wretched night. Noises in the hall kept awakening me, and when I sank back into sleep I was running through fire and struggling through curiously heavy water trying to escape some dreadful fate.

In the morning I felt fine. My doctor came and told me I apparently had not "ingested" much of the drugged food.

"I could have told you that."

"Smart aleck," he said, grinning. "Now I know you're going to live." Cute.

I got acquainted with my roommate over breakfast and we exchanged stories about why we happened to be where we were.

"Good heavens!" she said, when I had finished my recital. "Are you sure you're not making that up?"

Right after lunch I began getting anxious, but

it was an hour before my mother walked into the room.

She had a beautiful tan. Her long dark hair falling over her tanned shoulders and her hoop earrings — some new ones, I noticed — gave her a gypsy look which became her. Her eyes sparkled like a sun-drenched sea. You could tell just by looking at her that she was unforgivably happy.

I glanced beyond her and saw Kelly. "I thought he was going to drive the Thunderbird back?"

"When I repeated what you and Tony told me last night, Kelly said, 'Hell, I'll come back for the car.'"

I looked at my new stepfather warily. He was hanging back, keeping his big hands in his pockets. He looked huge and even more grossly freckled than when they left, but his expression was almost shy.

"Has Tony told you —" I began.

"Everything," my mother assured me, glancing at the sheer curtain between my bed and my neighbor's. "He and Marita met us at the airport."

I completely overlooked that "us" when I heard "Marita." "*She* met you? What did she want?"

"She wants to apologize to you, for one thing. She says she regrets very much what she did to you."

I studied my mother's face, trying to see in it what she was not telling me. I would have liked to hear that conversation. "What did Marita tell you that she did to me?" I asked, carefully.

"She admitted that she frightened you into leaving the apartment and moving in with her so she could more easily throw you and Rick together. She said she thought if she did that you would just naturally fall in love."

"Yeah, no one can resist her Rick." Then I realized what my mother had said. I sat straight up in my bed. "She was the prowler I had?" I asked, incredulous.

"Yes, that, too." The wary concern in my mother's eyes should have warned me, but what she said next came as a thudding shock. "She poisoned Tiger, Janice."

Marita, whom I had once so admired, had done that?

"Why is she admitting it?" I cried. "Why would anyone admit to doing a thing like that?"

Tiger had been trying to tell me that it was Marita in the woods above the hiking trail that day. Tiger had trusted her, because I did. And it was so calculated. She knew Tiger was my protection. She had deliberately frightened me, and then removed my protector. All in the name of matchmaking! She was as crazy as her nephew.

"She believes you blame Rick for it. She is as appalled as we are by what Rick attempted. But you're safe now, and Rick is not. Naturally, she is thinking of him. She hopes that by assuming some of the blame she can persuade you to drop the charges against him."

I looked at my mother, confused and troubled. Her face gave me no clue as to what she expected of me.

"I dictated a statement at the sheriff's office last night." I had lowered my voice, and I was aware of a sudden quiet on the other side of the curtain that concealed my roommate's bed. Now I knew why it was taking the nurse so long to do whatever she was doing there. It would be like this from now on, I knew, if I signed my statement.

"You . . . you can read it," I told my mother, shakily. "The sheriff said you might want to come with me today when I go back to sign it." I added, in a tone of challenge, "I told him exactly how it was."

My mother nodded.

Reluctantly, the nurse left the room. As if he had been waiting for this, Kelly approached my bed.

I was wondering what I could possibly say to him when he said, "I couldn't find a chocolate whip for you, Janice. Seems that even the *indios* are beginning to use electric beaters. So I brought you something else."

Out of his pocket he pulled a tiny white silky ball of a dog with hair falling every which way — fine hair so long I was not sure which end was which.

I opened my mouth.

"Ssh!" he warned. "I don't think the nurses

would approve." He extended his big hand and I took the ball of fluff gingerly.

"This is a dog?"

I heard my roommate's delighted laugh from behind the curtain.

"You don't have to keep it," Kelly assured me.

It sat on its hind legs in the palm of my hand and the fine silky hair parted to let one black eye stare at me. Suddenly a black button of a nose popped out of the fringe hiding its face, the ball wriggled ecstatically in my hands and a little pink tongue darted out to kiss my chin in a frenzy of love.

"Oh–h–h!" I cried, my heart dissolving. "I'm going to keep you, all right, you little rascal!"

My roommate sat up in bed and pulled back the curtain so she could see what I held. "If you don't, I will," she declared, laughing.

I cuddled the little thing in the curve of my neck where it just fit, and looked up at my new stepfather. He had known just what I needed to heal my hurt. Not even my father could have done better. I smiled at him. "I think I'll keep you, too, Kelly."

"You can call me Red," he said, with that big grin of his. He sat down beside my mother on the edge of the bed with his arm around her.

After that, we found we could talk more freely about what had happened. What surprised me was that my mother confirmed Rick's story about my father's half-brother.

"Your grandfather married again after his

first wife died. He married a widow with two boys, one older than your father and one about the same age. Hellions, both of them, your father told me. He never talked much about them, but I know that he left home when he was fifteen, after a terrible quarrel with your grandfather. He said he was never in touch with any of them after that."

"The younger half-brother must have been Rick's father. Rick said he was killed in Mexico," I told her. "It's the older one who is supposed to be leaving me a pack of money."

My mother shook her head in disbelief. "If there is any money in the family, I don't know anything about it."

"Rick's crazy, but Marita obviously believes it, too."

My mother turned to my stepfather. "This is killing her, Kelly. You know, last night I thought hanging would be too good for Rick. But today I am so happy that Janice is okay that I can feel sorry for Marita. Rick is like her own son."

"She said this morning that she will have to sell her ranch to pay for Rick's defense," my mother continued.

"Sell Casa de las Tres Hermanas?" I exclaimed. "That *will* kill her!"

"I doubt it," Kelly said drily. "Obviously, Rick's defense means still more to her."

"What will happen after I sign my statement?" I asked him.

When Kelly told me what I could expect — seeing lawyers, going to court, hearing Rick's lawyers try to convince a jury I could be lying, and then the jury maybe freeing Rick, maybe sending him to prison for years — I began to have butterflies in my stomach.

"Wouldn't it be better just to try to forget about it now? He didn't hurt me, after all."

But Kelly would have none of our qualms. "Nobody should get away with attempted murder," he said, firmly. "Rick cannot be excused from his actions because he failed to send you to your death in the canyon. If society excuses such behavior, it has no protection against madmen and criminals. Don't worry about your role in this, Janice. Your mother and I will be behind you all the way."

Greg appeared in the doorway, and my mother and Kelly stood up. Greg carried a bunch of flowers that almost hid his concerned face. He was wearing his ranger uniform and he looked trim and fit and quite handsome, even though he had a black eye with a cut above it.

My mother has good ESP. She introduced Greg and Kelly, then drew the curtain between my bed and my roommate's, and said, "Thank you, Greg, for everything. If it hadn't been for you —"

"— and the Crowders," I put in, smiling at Kelly to show him I remembered his advice.

"— and Sandy," Greg added.

"Well, we'll talk with you later, Greg," said my mother, her eyes very soft. "We want to see Janice's doctor now."

We giggled as Kelly took Fluff, that was the

name I had decided on, from me and gently tucked her back in his pocket, leaving his hand there. "She's chewing my finger," he explained. "It keeps her quiet."

"A man that lets a puppy chew his finger to keep her quiet can't be all bad," I told Greg when they had gone through my door.

He looked surprised. "Kelly's okay," he said, as if he wondered why I should doubt it. *Ah, but you didn't know my father*, I thought. And then I deliberately put the thought away. It was not fair to compare them. Kelly was Kelly. My mother was very happy, and he was behind me all the way. What more could I ask?

"You look pretty good in that uniform," I told Greg. "Did you work today? You couldn't have had much sleep!"

He grinned. "I got no sympathy because of that. But I got off early." He sat on the bed. "You look gorgeous in that hospital gown," he teased me. "In fact, you look gorgeous to me in just about anything." He dropped the flowers on the bed and kissed me.

I ran my finger lightly over the cut above his blackened eye. "You were wonderful," I said, softly. "I suppose to Marita it seemed so simple. She just knew no one could resist her Rick."

"Hah!" Greg exclaimed, very sure of himself. And why shouldn't he be?

"Do you know what Sandy told me last night while you were in the deputy sheriff's office? She said Marita and Weldon began planning to get that money for the Casa when Weldon saw

Rick's uncle's will. Marita even came to Santa Teresa to work just because she learned your mother had found a job there."

"So it was all calculated." Her interest in me. Her friendship. That was what hurt. "Even our meeting on the trail when she was hiking with Tony and I was walking my dog must have been planned."

I heard my mother's familiar step in the hall, and then her voice. She was returning with Kelly and my doctor, coming to release me.

Now I would have to go back to the sheriff's office. But my mother and Kelly would be with me. And Greg would be waiting to hear how it went. We kissed again, quickly.

Rick's trial is still months away. These summer evenings, I think sometimes about how all Marita's obsessive plans for saving her beloved Casa have gone astray. I am not an heiress, as far as we know, but I *am* in love with Greg, and he loves me.

It may not be forever — there is college ahead for both of us — but on the other hand, it might very well be!